Dear Reader,

Love at first sight can be a dream come true, but sometimes second chances can be even sweeter. This month, four breathtaking new romances from Bouquet prove it!

Veteran author Colleen Faulkner starts us off with the first in the new Bachelors Inc. miniseries, **Marrying Owen,** the story of an estranged couple forced into close quarters by a sudden storm—and ready to give love another try. Next up is the final installment in Vivian Leiber's the Men of Sugar Mountain trilogy, **Three Wishes.** When a man from her past returns to her small town, one woman wonders if he's now the key to the future she's always hoped for.

Sometimes romance blooms in the most unexpected places. That's what happens when the heroine of Wendy Morgan's **Ask Me Again** finds herself in a wedding party with the most boring guy she knew in college—and discovers he's become a fascinating and sexy man. Finally, Susan Hardy proves that every cloud really does have a **Silver Lining** when an accident that threatens everything one woman has leads her into the arms of a man who becomes the one thing she really wants.

Laughter, tears, desire, and most of all, love—Bouquet delivers them all. Why not give one a chance today?

Kate Duffy
Editorial Director

A WISH COME TRUE

He helped her find purchase and get out of the pond. She put the towel around herself and tucked it together atop her breasts. While she combed her hair, he smoothed out the plastic sheet and popped the air, filled up quickly to make a soft mattress. This he covered with a thin, blue blanket—pashmina, he would later explain—and then he grabbed a handful of blooms from the climbing wood anemone.

He scattered yellow blossoms on the bed he had made. The scent was not unlike the first day of a rose's opening.

"This is my altar," he said, lifting the wet curls from her shoulders. "And you, Zoe, you are who I worship."

A shiver went through her, not from cold, or fear, or even his touch. Just his words unleashed a craving for something that she couldn't even name, for she had never truly had it. When he finally——it seemed to be forever between his words and his actions—when he finally kissed her, she felt flame course through her. Shivers gone, replaced by raw heat. She dropped the comb and it went *ker-plunk* in the pond and disappeared.

"Win, make love to me."

"Let's take our time," he said. "And if you change your mind . . ."

She pulled out of his embrace and sauntered over to the flower-strewn bed, fully aware of his appraising eye. Coursing through her was a delicious sense of feminine power—all the better since his kisses had the power to make her throw away all that was right and proper. "I'm not going to change my mind. . . ."

THREE WISHES

Vivian Leiber

Zebra Books
Kensington Publishing Corp.
http://www.zebrabooks.com

Prologue

Teddy Sugar Mountain shoved the Request for Birth Certificate Copy form and a five-dollar bill across the counter.

"Please, ma'am, could you make this a rush order?" he asked the gray-haired woman at the computer screen. He danced from one sneaker to another. "I'm kinda in a hurry."

The woman, whose name tag cheerfully announced "Hi, My Name is Janet" squinted at the request.

"Young man, it takes twenty minutes to . . . oh, it's you."

Teddy blinked.

"Wondering how I knew you?" she asked, booting up the computer. "I remember all the interesting ones—women who claim their baby's father is Elvis or an alien, parents with names so long I can't fit it on the screens, the crazy ones who . . . oh, you're not like that. And I can see you've done all right—nice, polite, and I can tell just by the look of you you're going to be a babe magnet." She glanced at the form he had filled out. "How are your mothers?"

Mothers. The courthouse tucked away in Vail was an hour's drive from Sugar Mountain, and he had never met this Janet lady before—yet, she knew his name and the fact that he had an extra mother. Well, two extras. Three mothers in all.

"Paige is having another baby," he said. And Janet beamed. He continued, "She's married, you know, to TJ."

"Is it your first time being a big brother?"

"Oh, yeah," he said. The clerk was a stranger but she was awfully friendly. So friendly that he forgot that he was on a field trip with the Sugar Mountain Park District camp and that if he didn't get back upstairs to the courtroom where they were listening to a lecture on how the American judiciary system works, the counselors would notice he was gone. They might cancel the trip to the water park. They were like that when a kid messed up. "She's due in just a few months. The baby is kinda why I'm here."

"Ah, I thought this would happen one day," Janet said, and she keyboarded his name onto her screen. "Having a baby makes you feel like you're not the center of your mother's world. Or one of your mothers', at least."

"I hadn't thought about it that way—but now that you say so, I guess that's right. I feel a little jealous. But I don't mean to be that way."

"Perfectly natural," Janet said. She reached over

the counter and patted his hand. "And what about the blonde? Kate's her name, isn't it?"

"Yeah. She got married to Matt. He's the sheriff of Sugar Mountain."

Janet nodded.

"I told those girls that they would take that walk down the aisle."

"Zoe's not married," Teddy said. And he felt a rush of relief that at least that part of his family would stay the same. Funny, he was happy for his two moms. He liked TJ; he had always admired Matt, and being a big brother would be okay. Just so long as nobody expected him to change a diaper.

"I figured she would be the one to stay single. What with her mother to take care of and all," Janet said. She shoved her glasses to the bridge of her nose. "All right, Teddy, your birth certificate will come up on the printer in ten minutes. That's the best I can do."

Teddy glanced at the clock. When he had slipped out of the courtroom, he had told the counselors he needed to use the bathroom. Ten minutes? They'd be sending a search party. The water park would be a definite no.

"Don't bother printing it. I don't need to see it. I just want to know . . . you know . . . just wanna know . . ."

"Who your father is," Janet prompted.

"Yeah. But also I want to know which mom really is my mom."

Janet put her elbows on the counter and put her face up to Teddy's. So close he could smell the rose of her perfume and see that her lipstick didn't stay put but blended into wispy lines around her mouth.

"You have three wonderful women who have done all right by you," she said. "And they love you very much—I could see that when they came here to register your birth when you were just a few days old. That love they have for you—that's a darn sight better than a lot of kids get."

Teddy nodded guiltily.

"Maybe you should ask them the questions."

Teddy shook his head.

"I don't want to hurt them. I don't want them to think I don't like things the way they are. A lot of kids complain about their parents—especially the older ones—but I think my moms are great."

"You're scared if you ask which one is your birth mother that then two of them won't be your mother anymore?"

"Yeah, and I love all of them. I don't want to lose any one of them."

He made that declaration in the way all ten-year-old boys do—quickly, in an under-his-breath growl.

"All I can tell you, Teddy, is that all three women are listed as your mother."

"Really? Well, what about my father?"

She took her elbows off the counter and glanced at the computer screen.

"There's just one name. Skylar."

Skylar. His heart quickened, as if he had been skateboarding for hours in the hot sun. TJ? That'd be great, because he really liked TJ. But TJ would have said something—no way he'd be Teddy's dad and not want to claim him as his own. Or Matt? Being the sheriff's son might be cool. But there was also Win, who was long gone, and the brother who had died. James or Jack or John was his name. It was so darned confusing.

"Which one was it?" he asked.

Janet—he thought she was so nice—patted his hand again.

"I'm sorry I can't be more helpful. They told me a lot but that's the one thing they never answered. You should talk to them . . . Teddy . . . Teddy . . . don't run away."

He murmured a thank-you and then he bolted, charging up the marble stairs to the second-floor courtroom where his friends were listening to— make that, sleeping through—a black-robed woman's lecture on the American judicial system. He wiped away tears he couldn't have explained, took a deep breath, and slipped into the nearest empty bench.

That night, after the campers set up their sleeping bags on the floor of the Vail First Presbyterian Church basement, Teddy called his mother Zoe. Some of the other kids thought it wasn't cool to call home, but Teddy had never missed a night of talking with Zoe. He knew he wasn't calling because he needed to hear from her—although maybe when he was a kid, a little kid, that was true. No, he called because Zoe needed it. She missed him. She liked to hear about his day.

Each of his moms was special. Paige liked to take him places—when she'd worked in New York, they had done museums and zoos, like most families, but also the floor of the New York Stock Exchange and the Lotos Club, where real artists and writers hung out. Kate liked to read and talk and talk about what they'd read, and sometimes he'd thought she needed him the most—that is, until Matt came along.

But Zoe liked all the everyday stuff. Weird, but she liked to do his laundry. Liked to help him with his homework. Liked to be the one to take him to the doctor's office for a physical. When he was sick, she wanted to play checkers with him on his bed or read comics with him. She knew exactly how he liked his grilled cheese sandwiches, burnt with two slices of American, and she made it that way every time.

On his birthdays, Paige gave him presents picked out of catalogs that were exotic and wonderful, things he had never known he wanted so desperately until he saw them. Kate bought him tickets to the best games in Denver—and always included enough extras so that he could invite a few friends. But Zoe would always give him something that he had admired or longed for—even if he had never said a word, she seemed to know.

That night, when she picked up the phone, he told her about the trip to the courthouse (boring), the lecture on the judiciary system (stupid), the skateboarders the group had encountered outside as they were leaving (rad).

"Lemonade," he said before hanging up, and she said "lemonade, too," drawing her words out longer than he did. *Lemonade* was their code word, a way of saying *I love you* so that no one else would know that he was too old not to want to be loved and too young to be confident about saying the words.

One

"The presidency of the Women's Service Club is a position notoriously difficult to fill," Prudence Cruikshank prodded Zoe one honeydew summer morning when Teddy was away at camp. She had come to the rectory to sign up for the Seniors Dance to be held in the church basement on Saturday. She took particular care to tell Zoe that she was only going because her sister Emmeline wanted to shake a leg. But a ridiculous errand may be made worthwhile if a more worthy purpose is serendipitously achieved. "I have held the presidency more years than I care to recall and I need to pass the gavel to a younger, more vigorous woman. Do come to next week's luncheon meeting. After all, you have spent so many years nursing your mother and maintaining a home for Teddy, I think you need to live a little, get out more, go for it—as the young people say. Presidency of the Women's Service Club would be just the adventurous, fulfilling enterprise you need. And though you are just twenty-eight, you have a certain maturity so necessary to leadership."

"Thank you for thinking of me, Prudence," Zoe replied. "As for presiding over the club, thanks . . ."

"And it would only help your reputation," Prudence continued. "The cerebral lobe devoted to long-term memory is well developed in the people of this community." And here a long, bony finger with an emerald marcasite ring wagged inches from Zoe's face. "Most enlightened people, myself included, blamed Win Skylar for the episode, but . . ."

Zoe had endured this sort of comment many times, in silence and without indignation or the slightest desire to strike back—but there were limits.

". . . but no thanks."

Prudence gaped.

"Well," she said. And then she repeated the word *well* several more times. "Young lady, Teddy will be starting junior high school in the fall. Your mother, Lord bless her, has more years ahead of her than you or I could count using every one of our fingers and toes. It's true—she has more vim and vinegar than ten Cruikshanks. And this reverend, while nearly incompetent—no! no! don't defend him!—does not require more than thirty hours a week of your help. What do you propose to do with yourself?"

It was not a question Zoe hadn't asked herself, and Prudence Cruikshank had a distinct interrogatory style that made no allowances for the Constitution's Fifth Amendment right to zip one's lip.

"Miss Cruikshank, you know as well as I that many of your older members would not accept me at the helm of the Women's Service Board."

There. Zoe used the only weapon she had, a particularly satisfying weapon since it had so often been used to her detriment in other situations. Prudence sighed and pulled her white kid gloves from her pocketbook.

"I suppose there are a few who would not see the wisdom of my plan." And here Prudence's impeccable posture was compromised. Her brilliant idea, and all her ideas were by definition brilliant, had been given much thought. "But you could sway them. There are so many who have forgotten that Winfield boy. He's been gone for nearly eleven years. You've been a marvelous daughter, caring for your mother long after many lesser women would have found a nursing home. And Teddy is so even-tempered and intelligent that one nearly forgets his origins."

"But no one has forgotten my brief engagement to Rory Packer."

Prudence's shoulders fell low and rounded.

"Barely twenty-four hours," she clucked.

"Just long enough for a retraction to be printed. And he's never come back."

"Scandal is so wearying."

"So, I don't think I would be a good choice as president."

"I blame that Winfield boy. A Chevy Impala convertible. Red as the proudest rooster in a henhouse. No good could have come from that car. And that boy. He never did listen to reason."

"He had some different ideas," Zoe said mildly.

"Different! Bah! And you were but a child."

At the time, eleven years past, there had been no other topic at the Curl Up and Dye Salon, at the Stop'n'Shop, at the Little Lilac tearoom. Her mother, recently widowed, had cut out cautionary magazine articles of girls gone wrong and poignant "Dear Abby" letters. These she placed on Zoe's pillow, that being as much comment as she could muster. Several mothers of girls on the cheerleading squad demanded that Zoe be dropped or their own daughters would quit, but Zoe resigned so that the coach wouldn't have to choose. People stopped talking when Zoe entered the Little Lilac just before noon to work the lunchtime rush. Diners stared, seeming to expect that Zoe would impulsively yank open her starched white shirt to reveal . . . a black bra, no bra, or even a tattoo. Zoe quit her job because the owner, Libby Joyce, said the Little Lilac had its reputation to consider and a waitress who had just spent the night in the backseat of a Chevy Impala with Win Skylar was not an appropriate role model for the other staff.

Zoe had said, just once because she didn't feel it was dignified to have to repeat herself, that she and Win had fallen asleep in his car and were "just friends."

"I am so grateful that your father is not alive to hear you lie like that," her mother had said. "However, I can't send you to be counseled by the new reverend. He's utterly incompetent in matters such as this."

The new reverend offered her a job as his secretary, doing much the same work she had done for her father when he had been the shepherd of the Sugar Mountain flock. The new reverend's only comment on the matter was that as long as she apologized for having worried her mother by missing her curfew, all should be well.

He kept that kind, quiet sensibility, even when she brought home baby Teddy the next summer. The wisest Sugar Mountain matrons nodded and smirked—knew it all along, they told their friends. And the story about Kate and Paige sharing the title of mother—some folks said "HA!" even as others decided that perhaps Kate or Paige could have borne the cherub-faced child. Mrs. Kinnear took to her bed for a week, thinking she might die of shame—but when she held the infant Teddy in her arms, she slowly melted. It was a good five seconds before outrage and indignation were replaced by grandmotherly adoration. Not that she forgave her daughter for bringing him into the world without a father—no, not one bit! Reverend Martin got some indignantly worded mail, a few phone calls, and a trustee's demand that Zoe not be allowed back at her desk, but Reverend Martin was a man of several faults. He could not leave a pint of cherry chocolate ice cream unfinished; he rooted for the Chicago Bears when right-minded folks cheered the

Denver Broncos, and he believed it wasn't part of the job description of a minister to judge others.

"That's the good Lord's department," he had said mildly.

Since that time, three presidents had lived in the White House, *As The World Turns* had been canceled, several Trials of the Century had been tried, couples whose unions had been blessed in "Weddings of the Century" had divorced, and the Spice Girls had soared in the charts and broken up. In Sugar Mountain, folks got married, had babies, took jobs, lost jobs, took other jobs, built houses, sold them, and moved into new ones. Most people just didn't have the energy to be outraged that the church secretary was a single mother. Or more correctly, that she was one third of a single mother.

"Even if you could persuade the members, I still can't help you with your service board."

"And why ever not?"

"Because I've been thinking of taking up painting. I've always admired creative people. Not that I'm all that creative—just it might be fun."

Prudence reared up to her full, imposing height—somewhere between a large house plant and a two-drawer file cabinet—and made a squawk about models. Living ones. Nude ones. Tough to say which were worse—males or females in the nude. After all, Prudence and her sister Emmeline had spent a summer in the mid-1950s in Paris—they knew what artistic types could do.

"Landscapes," Zoe amended. "I can't draw well enough to do people."

"I suppose a well-bred lady can dabble in water-colors. And you can donate your work to the Women's Service Club Silent Auction Dinner."

"Oh, I don't think anything I'd do would be good enough to . . ."

"Zoe Kinnear, you do a good job at everything you put your mind to. I have no doubt that if you choose to do landscapes, they will be worthy of display."

After Prudence snapped her pocketbook shut and said good-bye, Zoe put away the folder for the Seniors Dance. Her desk was well-organized—paper clips in paper clip holders, pencils in pencil holders. Her attire was similarly well-organized, though it was one of the hottest days of August—T-shirts and cutoffs weather. Zoe wore a modest grey linen skirt with a honeydew-colored cotton twin set. She wore the cardigan with its sleeves tied around her neck. Her flat sandals opened to reveal buffed but unpolished toes. Her hair, a riot of coppery curls worthy of scandal, was pulled back into a tight chignon at the nape of her neck. The night before, she had soaked her hands in a solution of warm water and her mother's denture tablets to whiten her nails. And she wore only one item of makeup, a lipstick called Barely There Bronze, which was more barely there than bronze. She wore a lily of the valley perfume that was sold at the pharmacy in a no-nonsense bottle at a no-nonsense price.

As unvaryingly well-organized as her office and her appearance, so was Zoe's life. She cared for Mother and was surprised by Prudence's mention of a nursing home because she had, in fact, never thought of such a place for her mother. And she cared for her son Teddy—and as much as she wished for her mother, she wished doubly hard that Teddy feel loved.

Both these two wishes had—so far—been granted. At twenty-eight, Zoe had organized her desk, her appearance, her life to such a degree that she could put the remainder of her years on autopilot.

And that's exactly what made her so unnerved by Prudence Cruikshank's visit.

She went to the crafts shop that afternoon, bought supplies, and drove her unobtrusive green Toyota to a glade on Little Brown Mountain overlooking the village. She contemplated the church spire, the solitary stoplight, the tavern owned by Mayor Stern, the gabled roofs of Sugar Mountain's homes, even picking out the green-gabled house she had lived in all her life. She loved this town, felt there was something very nearly holy about its unchanging nature. Painting this view would be a pleasure even if she wouldn't want anyone to see her work. She watered some paints, lined up her brushes, and then felt a familiar light touch on the back of her neck.

She stilled.

Jack had only come to her a few times a year in the years since his death. And since it had been over ten years, she had developed many opinions about him.

He was a ghost.

He was a temptation.

He was an angel.

He was nothing more than a measure of her occasional disbelief that he could have been taken so young.

He was her misperception of physical sensations as mundane as the wind or the sun or the tug of a too-tight shoulder of her dress.

He was a symptom of PMS or post-PMS or having her period or not having her period.

Whoever, whatever he was, he was with her again.

She discounted the sensation, choosing this time to believe it was nothing more than the breeze.

She knew seeing Jack—well, it couldn't be called seeing because she had not once actually seen anything at all—but feeling Jack's presence should be something she should discuss with the reverend. But while the reverend was strong on empathy, helpfulness to the less fortunate, and a near total recall of his parishioners' names, he was not much on the infinite mysteries. She knew just what he'd do—take his glasses off, fog them, wipe them on his cardigan, and while trying to hide his bafflement, tell her it was just a psychological problem. The reverend was big on psychological problems.

She was sure she felt Jack push a strand of hair away from her forehead. The touch made her shiver.

She stood up, turned—and, as always, expected to see him—but of course, did not. The spruce trees waved gently in an empty breeze. The drooping white flowers of a lamb's head were crushed by only one set of feet. She was losing his scent, strongly masculine. She closed her eyes. His hand, sure and strong, curled around her waist to apply a barely there pressure on the small of her back. Her right hand came up to meet his fingers and she leaned her head forward until she felt his firm, unyielding shoulder.

The bells of the church began their two o'clock chime. The real bells in the spire were, of course, silent. There are not enough bell ringers in the country and not enough money to pay them. The Sugar Mountain Church of the Holy Comforter received a catalogue from a tape production company that recorded off a twelve-bell spire in Philadelphia. Zoe ordered the hours and single-tone half hours as well as appropriate melodies to jazz things up. She had a tendency to program in her favorites— "For All the Saints Who From Their Labors Rest" and "This Shepherd's Weary Work Untold"—too many times in a month.

"Amazing Grace" was another of her favorites and she remembered it had been Jack's.

She closed her eyes. The feeling lasted longer when she closed her eyes.

She felt Jack begin to sway, and she followed his lead, dancing slowly, achingly. She hadn't felt him in so long, not since just before Easter when she had felt a weightiness in the chair next to hers when she hosted the rummage sale organizational meeting. It had taken all her strength not to adjourn the meeting just so she could sit quietly in the church basement conference room.

I once was lost, but now am found. . . .

He would have been such a companion if he had lived. A good conversationalist. A hard worker. Sometimes he had had a manner that folks thought was too staid for one still in his twenties, but Zoe had appreciated the steady and unvarying nature of his mood.

It was such a tragedy that he was gone.

Jack took his hand away from the small of her back and covered her eyes. She took this to mean that she should not open them, that he would disappear if she did. Disappear *where,* she'd leave to ponder later. When his hand returned to her waist it felt even more real than ever before. It was not just that she felt his fingers' pressure on her flesh, but that the back hem of her linen dress rose up an inch as he pressed her near to him.

His other hand, holding hers—why, she could feel his pulse!

Could there be heartbeats in heaven?

Live for this now, she thought, and leave the theological debate for later. His breath, smelling sweeter than juniper and not as tart as spearmint leaves, touched her neck. She reached up, undid her chignon and let her hair cascade down around her shoulders. Her head fell backwards and he kissed her—yes, kissed her—lightly on her cheek and then seeking her lips as she blindly sought his.

Jack had never kissed her before. Never touched her for more than a few seconds, which could so easily be interpreted as a breeze or a falling leaf. He had never spoken to her from . . . well, wher-

ever he was. He only made his presence known by
a few clues and she could spend months afterwards
debating with herself whether or not she was crazy.

But this kiss was real. No doubts. No couldn't be's.
No going back to the office and saying to herself that
she needed to do those stress-relief breathing exer-
cises the reverend favored because she was going off
the deep end. His lips grazed hers and then slowly
tugged her lower lip as if she were a delectable fruit.
The teasing nature of his kiss aroused her hunger
and she threw her arms around his neck and
sought—no, demanded—more from him. She
opened her mouth to his tongue, she moaned as he
gave her more, she felt not a whit of righteousness
when the hand that did not steady her grazed the
hardened nipple of her . . .

"Oh, Jack," she groaned as their kiss ended. And
then he stiffened.

She opened her eyes.

Shoved with both hands.

Took one long, narrow-eyed, dangerous look.

He looked like Jack. Blond, cornsilk-soft hair that
fell in halo curls to his broad, climber's shoulders.
A strong jaw dominating a dimpled chin. Blue eyes
made bluer by contrast with a tan that didn't come
out of a bottle or a salon. Quite ordinary looking,
though, if you thought drop-dead-gorgeous men
were ordinary.

He carried himself like Jack, but with a telltale,
double-dare-you masculine confidence.

He kissed like Jack, although it had been eleven
years since she had actually kissed Jack, so she was

hardly in a position to know—except that Jack had never left her feeling as if she had been thoroughly, completely, and utterly kissed.

He was everything Jack had been. And if she could believe in ghosts or angels or the touch of a summer breeze, why shouldn't she believe this was Jack?

There was only one thing that made Zoe absolutely certain he was not.

A slight asymmetry of his nose, the result of a brawl in the alley out back of the drugstore started by a disgruntled boyfriend who had been displaced by Win Skylar in his girl's affections.

All this calculation took Zoe no more than a nanosecond.

What she did next surprised both her and the not-Jack whose arm still surrounded her waist.

She slapped his face. Hard.

Two

"Winfield Skylar, what do you think you're doing?"

He rubbed his jaw.

"You were doing it, too."

"I thought you were someone else."

"Who?"

"None of your business."

The bells on the church spire were finishing the final notes of "Amazing Grace."

"I didn't want to be kissed," she hissed.

He smiled. Didn't say the word *but*. Didn't say the word *you*. Didn't say the word *liked*. Didn't finish with the word *it*.

Didn't have to.

"Don't do it again," she warned.

"All right, next time I'll wait 'til you ask."

She gave him a heck-freezes-over look, picked up her paints, and dumped them, wet and messy, into her easel case. When the clasp broke and paint brushes and tubes spilled onto the grass and stone, she let out a shriek. Maybe not a shriek. More like a scream. No, maybe not a scream. But an expression of embarrassment mingled not a little with self-reproach and a lot of generalized anger. She crouched down to pick up her things. He squatted beside her, lazily picking up one brush, putting it in her case, and picking up another.

"You called me *Jack,*" he said.

She shoved paints, leaves, brushes into her case. She was so flustered, she would have shoved in a chipmunk that darted across her path, but it was too fast for her.

"You heard me wrong."

"No, no, I'm positive. You said *Jack.*"

"Oh, no, I wouldn't say *Jack,*" she lied, and because she was unused to lying, a flame-hot defensive blush ran up her cheeks. "Because you are not Jack. I must have said smack or whack, which is what I intended on doing to you once you stopped taking advantage of me."

"No, you said *Jack.*"

She uttered an oath, a very minor one in the constellation of oaths. In fact, an oath that was so mild that it could hardly carry weight in a world weighed down with invectives.

"Darn it!"

And then she stood up, holding her easel case as best she could.

"It's not an unheard of phenomenon to think a departed friend is . . ." Win said.

Painting landscapes now seemed to her to be the stupidest idea Prudence Cruikshank had ever had.

Even worse than the presidency of the Women's Service Club.

"Win, I didn't say Jack."

"Okay, okay. I believe you."

She waited.

"And I apologize."

She nodded.

"I accept your apology for slapping me . . ." And here he paused as she opened her mouth to protest. ". . . and extend to you an invitation to go dancing again."

"I think that would be unwise," she replied frostily.

"I don't see anything sparkling on your left hand, so I assume you're not married."

"I really must get back to work."

"Does *I really must get back to work* mean you're not married?"

"All right, fine, so you want to know—I'm not, as it so happens, married."

She hazarded the briefest glance at his calloused hands. She wouldn't have guessed him to be the settle-down kind of guy anyway.

"Me, neither," he said. "Should we do this tomorrow? Same time, same field?"

"In your dreams."

"I was in yours for a moment."

She strode down the path with stately dignity. And turned around before she had gone ten steps.

"Hey, what are you doing here now, after all these years?"

"Have to be someplace in the universe."

"You were always a smart aleck. I mean, where have you been?"

He shrugged. The answer would be long and adventure-filled. He was willing; she wasn't.

"How long were you watching me before you . . ."

"Just a few minutes. You were dancing like a woman who wanted a man to dance with. Church still disapproves of dancing?"

"That was a long time ago, before you and I were born."

"Your mother disapproves of dancing."

She bit her lip. Of course, her mother didn't care that their denomination had, in the mid-1950s, declared that drinking (in moderation), dancing (in moderation), and R-rated movies (for adults) were not sins. Although she was relieved that bridge had been taken off the big sin list.

"Did you see anything?" She asked. "Like a bright light?"

"There's the sun."

"No, that's not what I'm talking about. Did you feel anything?"

"I felt you. You were soft and warm and just the right size for a man to . . ."

She shook her head primly.

"That's not it, either."

"I felt your lips. You kiss like you haven't had a good kiss in years," he observed.

"Winfield!"

"Well, have you?"

"Have I what?"

"Been kissed?"

"That's none of your beeswax."

"Agreed. But still."

"So, you didn't see or feel anything unusual?"

"Nothing more unusual than a woman dancing by herself in the middle of a field to the bells of the church."

She had nearly reached the patch of junipers before she thought of something else.

"When did you get here?"

"Yesterday."

"How long are you staying?"

"Just a few days. I have some things to settle up and then I'm gone again."

"Well, good. I mean, go. I mean, have a nice visit."

"I meant what I said about dancing."

No, no, she shook her head.

"I could take you to the mayor's tavern. He can't be any worse at playing the trumpet than he was when I lived here. And we don't have to eat the onion loaf. In fact, I won't eat it if you don't. It'll be better that way."

"I'm very busy," she said with just the right amount of starch so that he should know that the only reason that she wasn't saying *no* was because she didn't wish to appear rude.

He reached to tip his cap before realizing his head was bare.

She charged into the juniper-bordered path.

"Such a goody-two-shoes."

"Better a goody-two-shoes . . ." she muttered under her breath, ". . . than a . . ."

What would you call Win Skylar—especially when the word *devil* has already been taken? She looked over her shoulder. The glade was empty.

Win hiked further up the path until he was certain she could not see him. Then he sat down on a rocky ledge overlooking the village.

Damn stupid, that's what he was.

He shook his head.

Grabbing Zoe alone in the middle of nowhere, planting a kiss on her lips—he had probably scared her half to death. And how was that for a greeting after eleven years? He supposed it didn't matter that his social graces were so rusty. After all, he was just here for the money. And to cut his ties to Sugar Mountain, once and for all.

The morning after leaving the glade, she was staring open-mouthed and wide-eyed at the morning news when she realized she was wondering if she would see him again before he left town. The doorbell rang. She flipped off the television guiltily, nearly knocking over her empty coffee cup, and opened the front door to Kurt the mailman.

He held a large white box tied with a red satin ribbon.

"Good morning, Kurt."

He tipped his cap perfunctorily.

"Do you know it's a federal offense to deliver anything to a residential premises in a mailbox?"

"Uh, no, actually, Kurt, I didn't."

"A residential mailbox is actually federal property, not for the use of whomever and whatever."

"Okay."

"You tell whoever gave this to you that he or she is not supposed to put things in the mailbox. They're interfering with my proper functioning as a federal employee. Got it?"

"Sure, Kurt. I'm so sorry, I don't know who . . ."

"Well, open it, Miss Zoe."

She pressed her lips together. Kurt called married women *Mrs.*, young women by their first names, and elderly women *Miss*. She believed he thought himself gentlemanly.

"Zoe, is that the mail?" her mother called from the living room. Mrs. Kinnear liked catalogs and you-might-have-won letters.

"Yes, Mother, I'll be bringing it right in."

"Mrs. Kinnear, there's a package for Zoe," Kurt yelled past Zoe's shoulder. "But the sender put it in the mailbox and . . ."

Mrs. Kinnear hobbled to the door. She was a large woman, inclined to give a first impression not unlike a stately hippopotamus. She sometimes used a cane, although her doctor had specifically told her she did not need one. And she sometimes asked Zoe to drive her to the grocery store, though it was just a half block away and her doctor had told her she needed exercise. Mrs. Kinnear gratefully accepted Kurt's proffered elbow to steady herself and she regarded the white box with some suspicion.

"It's not your birthday. It's not a holiday."

"No, Mother, I'll just take this box inside," she said. She knew that not opening the box would be denying Kurt one of his greatest pleasures. He was the sort of mailman who delivered Christmas cards and waited on the porch for you to open them so he could admire the pictures. And you'd do it because he shivered so in the cold.

"How do you know it's for Zoe?" Mrs. Kinnear asked.

"Because it has an envelope taped to it," Kurt said, and he yanked the gift insert off the box.

"These days, you can't be too careful," he said, hanging onto the box. "If you don't know who sent the package and you weren't anticipating a package, you should exercise extreme caution." Zoe tugged and he tugged back with his free hand until Mrs. Kinnear joined in.

"Kurt, this is Sugar Mountain. Nothing ever—"

"A person who would violate federal law by placing a private package in a mailbox is the same sort of individual who would—"

"Zoe, Kurt's right—we don't even know who sent this to you."

He tugged. Zoe tugged. Her mother, being the strongest of all three and not weighted down by a full morning's mailbag, tugged hardest. Hard enough that the box slipped out of the mailman's hand, but at that moment, it also slipped from Zoe's and her mother's hands. The box dropped to the front porch, spilling out its contents—white tissue and a slithery mass of fire-engine red.

"Here, let me."

"No, that's all right."

"I can pick it up."

"Oh, my heavens!" Mrs. Kinnear cried out.

"I got it."

"No, really."

When the dust cleared, Kurt and Zoe were holding between them a skimpy red dress with delicate spaghetti straps and a shamelessly fringed hem. It was made of a silk that no Sugar Mountain resident, Zoe in particular, had ever seen. The sort of silk used for Indian saris and temple curtains, the silk used to upholster the raj's chaise, the silk used to curtain the entrance to a Turkish pleasure dome.

All in all, a dress that would be perfectly suitable if, say, Zoe decided to become a Las Vegas showgirl or were making a lamp shade for a bordello.

Kurt whistled.

"Maybe this was meant to be delivered to Kathy Cook."

Kathy was the Kinnears' next-door neighbor. At forty, she had sworn off men—but not before four husbands, two live-in boyfriends, and an enduring adoration for Mick Jagger that ended abruptly when he moved back in with his ex-wife Jerry Hall.

"Kurt, you take this to Kathy's house right now," Mrs. Kinnear demanded. "No one would send Zoe such a dress."

Zoe touched her forehead.

"Oh, no, I think I know who . . ."

"Let me look at that note," Mrs. Kinnear said.

Zoe and Kurt dropped to their knees, scrambling

for a sliver of paper that had fluttered out from the envelope.

"Dancing tonight," Kurt read and then he stared aghast at Zoe. "Signed, *Win Skylar.*"

Zoe yanked the dress out of his hands and snapped up the note.

"I can't imagine why he'd send me such a thing."

"I can," Kurt said with the bland confidence of a man of the world.

"I didn't even know he was still in town," she added. "I thought maybe he had already left."

"When did you see him?" her mailman and mother cried out as one.

"On Little Brown Mountain, when I was painting."

"That's not a fit hobby for a woman. The Cruikshank sisters tell some mighty scandalous stories about painters they met in their summer in *Par-ee.*"

"What's he doing back in town?" Mrs. Kinnear demanded.

"He's staying at the apartment over the Skylar Sports Shop," Kurt said. "Remember, he still has an inherited interest in the place."

"Oh, dear, I hope he's not staying."

"Mother, please go sit down. I'll take care of this."

"I wish you would have married Rory," Mrs. Kinnear sighed. "He was such a nice boy. Well-mannered. Thoughtful. Patient. Gentlemanly. And he would have settled you down."

"I am settled down," Zoe said, then added under her breath, "I'm so settled down, it's scary."

"Mrs. Kinnear, let me help you," Kurt said. "You look a little peaked."

"That man being back in town is going to wreak havoc with my blood pressure. Children are a great trial, you know."

"Oh, yes, Mrs. Kinnear. I've got two of my own. I owe all my grey hair to them."

Kurt aided Mrs. Kinnear in her stately progress to the living room couch.

"I thought we were over that Winfield episode," she said. "You don't have to explain. I understand. I've always thought you were a good girl. I had hoped that all I gave you as a mother would make up for all you didn't get because of not having your real mother. . . ."

"You are my real mother," Zoe said wearily, for they were on familiar ground.

"We tried for so long and I wanted a child so badly. . . ."

"Mother, don't you think you're overreacting a little?"

"I'm trying to protect you."

"Kurt, I think it's time for you to go," Zoe said.

"Surely, Miss Zoe," he said and tipped his hat. But Mrs. Kinnear was not finished.

"We waited so long to adopt, thinking we would do it the natural way and then being disappointed in that. When you came to us, just a little squalling bundle in a pink blanket, I was so tired, so much more tired than a woman of twenty getting up with her baby. And then when you were a toddler, so quick and so energetic, I couldn't keep up. Well, if I had just been a better mother maybe you wouldn't have . . ."

Kurt eased towards the door, but not before leaning into Zoe's ear.

"I heard all the talk about that red Impala. I've been one of those who thought all along that Win Skylar deserved a good whipping—if there were someone who could catch him."

Mrs. Kinnear closed her eyes and placed her fingers at her temples to ward off a headache.

"Nothing happened," Zoe said.

Kurt nodded so vigorously that his chins doubled and tripled and quadrupled, even though he was not an ounce over the government's recommended weight for postal carriers of his height.

"Sure, I know. It's all right. You're too good, and that's part of why a man like Win can take advantage of you. You can't imagine how others could act with reckless disregard for the feelings of others because you would never be able to do that yourself. And then there's the issue of him being the father of—"

"Nothing happened."

"Sure," Kurt said, wounded. He reared up. His summer-weight uniform's epaulets fell into a straight line, accentuating his shoulders.

"I'll return the dress to him immediately," Zoe said.

"He's receiving mail at the Skylar Sports Shop. Does not take residential delivery. If you package it and address it properly, I could drop it off," Kurt offered and added in a whisper, "I wouldn't even charge you postage, seeing as this is a sensitive matter and you didn't want the dress in the first place."

The notion of Kurt on his rounds with dress in hand was too much.

"No, I'll take care of it."

His face fell.

"Kurt, you aren't going to say anything to anyone, are you?"

He reared up.

"As a postal employee, I take an oath to respect the confidentiality of my customers. By the way, here's your mail. It's just bills, but looks like you need to renew your subscription to *Newsweek*. And your mother won a Caribbean cruise."

"She's just a semifinalist. She's always a semifinalist. Everyone's a semifinalist."

"Aw, jimminy, I was thinking she had finally won this time."

She thanked him, took their mail, picked up the white cardboard gift box, and glanced up from the pile of tissue paper just as Kurt said hello to her neighbor Mrs. McGillicuddy across the street.

Mailman and retired teacher huddled together, solemnly nodded several times, looked over their shoulders at Zoe, and brought their heads so close to one another's that they could have been mistaken for Siamese twins.

That was when Zoe calculated that she had until noon, give or take ten minutes.

Kurt would complete his deliveries, and every resident of Sugar Mountain would believe themselves to be in full possession of the facts. And those that didn't have a sufficiently developed memory lobe in their cerebral cortex would have plenty of remedial instruction from neighbors, friends, and family.

She grabbed her purse, and her keys and told her mother she had a very important errand.

It wasn't the first time she had had a problem with runaway "facts."

Three

The little bells over the door of the Skylar Sports Shop announced her arrival. Win glanced up from his laptop, which he had positioned on the counter by the cash register.

"Why, Zoe, it's a pleasant . . ."

She marched up to the counter and dropped the box on top of a pile of receipts from a snowshoe supplier.

". . . surprise."

"While I appreciate the sentiment."

They each stared at the box.

"You don't like the dress."

"It's a beautiful dress but that is not the point."

"What is the point?"

"I cannot accept such a present and besides . . ."

"Why not?"

"It's not appropriate."

She noticed he had looked up, but was not looking at her. Rather, his blue eyes, set deep beneath full brows, widened. He was mesmerized by a vision just beyond her right shoulder. She looked down

at herself. Not a smidgen of dandruff. She waved
a hand in front of his face, but he did not blink.
She turned her head, following his gaze—first to a
display of backpacks, which could hardly be of such
hypnotic power, and then to the window, where a
horrifying assembly had developed on the sidewalk.

"Oh, no," she said. "I'm too late."

Three middle-aged matrons and Mr. Eckhardt
from the hardware store had never looked more
menacing.

"Appropriate is a word you used to use a lot,"
Win mused, continuing to stare out the window. "I
never did figure out why you liked it so much."

"It's a very useful word when conducting one's
life in a small town," she said.

"What do you think they're looking at?"

"They're looking at us."

The Skylar Sports Shop was a no-nonsense store
that offered a commendable selection of baseball
mitts, basketball jerseys, and the essentials of a rug-
ged life enjoyed by the residents of Sugar Mountain who lived beyond the downtown's gabled
Victorian homes and modern split-levels. The
clothing was unfashionable but durable—overalls,
long underwear, ski pants, gloves and parkas. Kero-
sene, road salt, and antifreeze were sold in bulk.
Lawn mowers, bikes, trikes, and snowmobiles were
parked against the back wall. None of the sun-
glasses cost more than an Andrew Jackson, and
none had been featured in a blockbuster summer
hit. The jeans were clean, unfaded, and unrepen-
tantly intact.

It was not a store for window shopping—it was a store for coming in with a list. And yet, at this very moment, five Sugar Mountain residents stood spellbound by the window display of zinc-oxide sunblock that could double as bug repellent.

Of course, not so spellbound that they couldn't spare a gander at the counter. Zoe noted that the three women all lived on Kurt's morning route, down Cherry Street, across Oak to Locust Avenue. Mr. Eckhardt's hardware store was on the corner of Locust and Cherry.

"Take the dress."

"But, Zoe, it's just a gift. I didn't mean anything. I'm only in town for a couple of days and I thought maybe, well . . ."

"It's far too expensive."

"It was about three dollars, American. Got it at a street market in Delhi, been lugging it around in my backpack for two years wondering why I wanted it so bad, whom I'd bought it for, and when I saw you, I realized you had been in the back of my mind all along. It's perfect for you."

"It's red."

He took his eyes off the window. Brought his eyebrows together as he puzzled over the dress. He looked up. His eyes were as mesmerizing as the crowd outside. She had remembered him as being handsome enough to be trouble, through and through; but although there were a few fine lines when he smiled and his mouth had the set of a man who had seen his share of danger, Winfield Skylar was still the kind of man that could give Hollywood "it" boys a run for their money.

She sighed.

"It'll be beautiful with your hair."

"Redheads can't wear red."

"The best ones can."

"It's too short."

He leaned over the counter.

"You should show off your legs."

"I can't accept it."

"You were beautiful when you were dancing on the mountain, and it was as if you wanted a man to hold you."

"I did have a man to hold me!" she said. Well, actually, that's what she *wanted* to say, but instead she merely pushed the dress across the counter as if every inch she pushed would persuade him where words had failed.

"Zoe, come on. It's T.G.I.F."

T.G.I.F.?

"Thank God it's Friday," he prompted.

As with many women who work outside the home, Friday night was catch-up night. There was no T.G. about it. Laundry, bills, dishes that hadn't gotten done on Thursday, newspapers from the day before, recycling bins to fill, toys to pick up, lawns to mow.

She noticed just the slightest scent of rosewood and lime. He smiled a smile that had gotten him everything. Everywhere. Every time. She felt herself weakening.

"Come on," he said. "You're over twenty-one, right? And you're single, right? So why not?"

What could be so wrong about an adult woman, single at that, with her child off at camp, her mother—well, Friday evenings Mother liked television—what would be the harm just this once? With just this one man?

It was the second question rather than the first that clinched it. She had disapproved of everything he had done in high school. Had told him, too, that coloring inside the lines was the only way to deal with crayons, that one should never run with scissors in one's hand, and that rules were meant to be . . . well, followed. How could a world exist without order? she had asked. And how could a person live without breaking a few rules along the way? he had replied.

Maybe she wasn't so right, she thought, savoring the idea of this once, just this once . . .

A squeaking noise. She looked back at the window. Kurt had joined the assembly and had pressed his face so far into the window glass that his nose was twisted nearly back into his cheek.

"I really can't," she said. "Take the dress."

"It's them, isn't it?" He gestured toward the window.

"As a matter of fact, no. It's me," she said. "I'm busy. Have a lot to do this evening. Gosh, I just don't know how the time goes by so quickly. Maybe we'll get together sometime while you're in town."

"Zoe."

"Okay, it's a little bit of them. Yes, all right, think what you want, it is them."

"They don't forget, do they? They're like elephants."

"They remember everything." Zoe nodded. "Even the stuff that wasn't true."

"And a red dress would only make them think they'd been right about you all along."

"That's right. But there's a little more in between."

"Like what?"

She pursed her lips together.

"They were wrong," Win reminded her. "We didn't do a damn thing in that car."

She slid the white box across the counter.

"Thank you, Winfield. For thinking of me."

He sighed.

Two years in a backpack was a long time for a dress to so wait patiently, only to be rejected.

"I'll only take it back if you have dinner with me."

She stared heavenward.

"Just for old time's sake."

"I don't think that's a wise idea."

"Otherwise I'll put it back in your mailbox."

She thought of Kurt. And her mother. And the handsome man who could be so charming—and so contrary. He had said he was leaving in a few days . . . It would just be once.

Once was always enough to get her into trouble.

"I'll call you," she said.

"No, because you'll just put it off until it doesn't happen. Are you free tonight?"

"I have stuff to finish up at the office."

"After work?"

"It'd be late."

She was surprised by the naked disappointment on his face. Why should he care whether she went to dinner with him? There were so many other women who would gladly sit across from him to eat a meal or just to stare at his handsome face.

"Six o'clock," she blurted. She added the only place in town she could think of. No way would she drive with him to Breckenridge or Iron Horse or any of the neighboring towns that were forty or fifty miles away. "The Little Lilac."

"Not there. How about the mayor's tavern? Oh, no, you don't have to say it—inappropriate."

"It's not my kind of place."

"Okay, how about dinner at your house?"

She glanced at the window.

"You were a good friend to me. I just want a friendly dinner with you. I won't even kiss you again."

She closed her eyes against his words, knowing him so well even after so many years. He was outside again, outside looking in. Feeling unwelcome and unwanted.

"Sure, Win," she said, turning and giving him her best smile as she shook her head. "It's wonderful to have you here. I'll have dinner with you. But let's do it at the Little Lilac."

She felt a great relief, and not just because his

face broke into a smile that was at once boyish and proud.

"Six o'clock. I'll try to remember not to tell the owner that I like women in white rubber-soled shoes."

She did a double take.

"Just joking. I know, I know—inappropriate. How did you ever bring yourself to be a friend of mine?"

"Win, I always thought you were a good person."

The bells rang with inappropriate cheer. She stepped out onto the sidewalk, nodding a curt hello to several people whose mouths were opened in fly-catching awe.

"You were the only one who did," Win said, and returned to the profit-loss figures on his laptop. He glanced up only when the folks on the sidewalk had scattered like sparrows.

On his sixteenth birthday, Winfield Skylar stopped going to school. In a big city, that wouldn't have been enough to raise a jaded eyebrow. In Sugar Mountain—scandalous—considering that the high school graduation rate was 100%.

The principal came to the Skylar house to talk him out of it. After all, he had such potential; he just didn't apply himself. If he was determined to smoke, he could just go outside between classes. As for challenging the teachers on their lessons, well, that was okay, part of the educational process as long as he did it respectfully. But the principal left the Skylar home with tears in her eyes and told her husband she had just lost the brightest student she had ever known. Winfield wasn't graduating.

Mayor Stern collared Win one day in the parking lot of Lakeside Foods, telling him that he'd better not get into trouble with drugs, delinquency, and, by the way, what was that book he was holding, with the naked guy on the cover? The naked guy was Michelangelo's *David* and the book was an account of Renaissance artists, which Win offered to loan the mayor, but the mayor liked detective novels so he declined.

"I don't want any misbehavin'," he said, wagging a finger at Win. "Do you have something to do with yourself?"

"Yes, my brother Jack gave me a job. I'll be guiding the treadmill tourists on climbs."

"Not on my mountains you won't," the mayor warned—and he warmed to his rant even as Win said, "No, sir, we'll be working in Vail." The mayor continued, "Jerks thinking because they spend a few hours a week in a health club that they've got what it takes to climb a fourteen-hundred-foot slope." The mayor let loose a string of oaths before remembering he was in the presence of a minor. "Good thing Jack's in charge of you. He'll set you on the straight and narrow."

"I doubt that."

"And by the way, you didn't throw mud balls at Tom Barron's windows, did you?"

"No, I didn't."

"Well, I'll be damned—sorry, darned—if I can

figure out who did. If I find out you're lying to me . . ."

Win's mother, the widow of Skylar Sports Shop's owner, said she hadn't expected much more from him because he had been trouble from the moment he was born.

"You're not hanging around this house if you're not in school," she said.

It was Jack who persuaded her to let Win move into the apartment above the shop.

Daughters were warned that they were not to keep company with Winfield Skylar—but they did anyway. Sons were told no hanging out with that kid—but Win wasn't much for hanging out anyway. Tom Barron told everyone in town that he was sure Win was the perpetrator of the mud ball incident.

Win looked the part—he had a tattoo of a Sacred Heart on his left arm. He wore his hair just too danged long. He didn't go to church on Sunday. He peppered his talk with words not fit for ladies, children, and dogs. He roared down Main Street in a Chevrolet Impala that was painted a made-for-trouble red.

Only Mrs. McGillicuddy had a good word for him because he still mowed her lawn every week during the summer and shoveled her walk in winter.

But even she admitted she wouldn't let her daughter near the window when he worked.

"He takes his shirt off and you can see his . . . muscles," she told the head-shaking members of her bridge group one afternoon after she invited

Win inside to take his pay. "You'll notice he has a very tight butt."

"I'd notice no such thing!" Prudence Cruik-shank had replied sharply.

Zoe Kinnear, daughter of the late Reverend Kin-near, lived under tight restrictions. No dresses above the knee, no tight jeans, no dating, no ciga-rettes, no card playing, no movies that didn't have a big fat G in their advertisements, no dancing, and most certainly no associating with the likes of Win-field Skylar.

So how did it come to pass that they would be discovered by Mr. Smith on a cold November dawn on the fallow fields of his farm in the back seat of a Chevrolet with their arms wrapped around each other and their stockinged feet sticking out from under one of Mrs. Skylar's fine, handmade quilts?

"It was my fault," Win muttered at his laptop. He had said it then, said it since, said it now. "I should have taken her home. Early. Before she fell asleep. Before the sun came up."

Any of those options would have been rational, reasonable, and wouldn't have had such conse-quences.

But even the strongest man finds it hard to give up heaven, and heaven was a red Impala that night.

Four

The busiest corner of Sugar Mountain has a stoplight that was installed several years ago in a day-long ceremony in which Mayor Stern dug the first shovel of dirt and announced that Sugar Mountain was now a metropolis. The stoplight is largely decorative, not because folks don't obey traffic regulations but because the lights don't change. Instead, only the red light blinks on and off, on and off, all night and day—although the yellow and green lights are ready in case a sudden transportational surge turns Chestnut and Elm streets into a snarl.

Drivers come to a full stop, edge tentatively into the intersection, wave seniors and bike-riders through, and only then, if nobody else objects, they slip mildly through to the other side. On this night, with Sheriff Matt on his honeymoon for one more day, everyone took particular care to respect the other person's right-of-way, so much so that each car lurched and abruptly stopped several times before making it across the divide with considerable hand gesturing along the lines of "you go ahead" and "oh, no, I couldn't possibly" and "ladies first."

On the four corners stand the ivy-covered library, the squat cement post office, Fred's Gas Station, and the Little Lilac Tea House, which does not serve tea and looks more like a brick cube with a picture window than any other house in town.

The Little Lilac is run by Mrs. Libby Joyce, whose face bears a striking resemblance to the cattle her husband raises on their ranch just outside town limits. Her sole vanity is to wear her taffy-and-grey-colored hair at a length that reaches her considerable hips. When she works, she wears a ponytail low on her neck and some folks swear that when she's angry—a busboy sloppy with the coffeepot, a waitress who has confused her customers' orders, a cook too slow with the spatula—Mrs. Joyce's hair twitches not unlike the tail of a cow swatting a mosquito on its rump.

Certainly, Mrs. Joyce's ponytail twitched and reared that evening, when, precisely at the hour of six, a bright red convertible confidently swaggered through the intersection and parked in front of her door.

"Lookie who the cat dragged in," she said as Winfield Skylar came in. "I heard you were in town. But I couldn't believe it. How long you stayin'?"

"Just for a few days, Mrs. Joyce," Win said easily. "I don't have a reservation but . . ."

They both perused the sullenly hot dining room. Mrs. Joyce rued the fact that she had not purchased RESERVED cards at the restaurant supply company in Boulder where she shopped. She would not have been above placing one of these cards on each of the four booths, two tables, and six round leather stools at the counter. This was the man who had seduced her best waitress, Zoe—and Mrs. Joyce was a grudge holder.

"Suit yourself," Mrs. Joyce said, heaving herself up from her elbows-on-the-counter pose. She poured a glass of tepid water from a pitcher and slapped a menu on the counter.

Ignoring these concessions to hospitality and commerce, Win sauntered to the corner booth, taking the seat that allowed him a view of the door.

"Booths are for more than one person at a time."

"I'm expecting someone," Win said.

Mrs. Joyce brought him the water and a menu.

At that moment Mrs. Joyce's ponytail reared up. Her head turned to the door when the cheerful bells announced her newest customer. Her nostrils flared. Her how-now-brown-cow? eyes widened. She mouthed the "You the one who ordered this heat?" that was her friendliest greeting during August. But at the same time she had an itching to add "get out, Zoe, now, while you've got a chance."

In every respect but one, Zoe looked as impeccably virtuous as a saint who needed protections against a charming but reckless devil. Her hair was slicked back into its familiar bun—nary a single wisp astray. A baby pink tan ran across her nose and cheeks, dusted only by nature's powder of barely there freckles. Her dress was shapeless, as if made by two oversized rectangles of beige linen sewn together; and yet, this sack of a dress was precisely the problem.

The offensive fabric and the back light from the glare from the windshield of Win's car combined to create a silhouette that was positively indecent.

Zoe had legs. Legs like a highway connecting to her hips and a waist that brought a four-lane down to one smooth ribbon of flesh. A cool stretch of body that made Win say "Wow" with a breath he hadn't even known he had been holding in.

"Harrummph!" Mrs. Joyce said.

She had long admired Zoe—or felt sorry for her and exasperated by her weakness for Win, depending on how one defined these terms. It was a feeling not unlike what Mrs. Joyce felt for certain made-for-TV movie heroines. Man does woman wrong; she pays for it dearly, but the heroine remains cheerful and stoic. This feeling had often led Mrs. Joyce to slice Zoe an extra-large piece of pie for her luncheon desserts.

But Zoe looked as if she were bringing trouble on herself, which made-for-TV heroines only did once.

"Hello, Mrs. Joyce," Zoe said cheerily, not noticing that the restaurateur's goodwill had slithered out the door behind her. "Looks like you have our table ready."

Mrs. Joyce looked at Win, who was rising from his seat to greet his guest. "Two menus, huh?"

As Win and Zoe awkwardly greeted each other,

a waitress poked her head out the swinging kitchen door.

" 'S'all right," Mrs. Joyce said. "I'll take care of these two."

"These two" said in the same way a hardened detective might refer to his beat's most heinous criminals.

It was, after all, understandable if ten years before one Little Lilac waitress had fallen astray to the charms of Win Skylar, but to have two of her waitresses do so would suggest Mrs. Joyce was careless. And she was not. The waitress retreated. The kitchen doors swung back and forth and stilled. Mrs. Joyce hoisted her frame onto a stool behind the counter, put her elbows down, and rested her chin on her hands.

"So . . ." Zoe said, and she glanced at the immovable Mrs. Joyce. "You're only in town for a few days?"

"That's right," Win said. "I have a ticket out of Denver for day after tomorrow."

"Hmmm."

"Harrummph," Mrs. Joyce said.

"You won't have a chance to see TJ and Matt," Zoe said. "TJ's in New York with Paige on a business trip."

"Yeah, I heard they were married. 'Sabout time."

"And they're expecting."

"Great!"

Mrs. Joyce sneezed. Win and Zoe blessed her in unison.

"And Matt's still on his honeymoon in California until tomorrow," Zoe said.

"Well, you'll have to send my best wishes to both couples."

"You don't want to stay and see them?"

"Really, it's all right. I don't think they'd be interested."

"Of course they would!"

"Harrummph!" Mrs. Joyce said.

Zoe glanced at Mrs. Joyce.

"What about seeing your mother?" Zoe asked.

"That's a tough one."

"She's not well."

"What's the matter?"

"I think it's agoraphobia," Zoe said. "Some kind of post-traumatic—"

"She won't leave the house," Mrs. Joyce said.

"Maybe I should let her be," Win said. "I have to get back. I'm a guide in Bhutan for now. Anyhow, I dropped off wedding presents at Paige's mom's house because I don't know where they're living . . ."

"The green house on the corner of Birch and Salem. It's where Mr. Petrie lived."

". . . and another package at Matt's office."

Mrs. Joyce coughed.

"They're just two small loose stones," Win said, looking directly at Mrs. Joyce as if that might intimidate her into giving them some privacy. But the counter had two smooth, oval depressions, and when Mrs. Joyce's elbows found these familiar grooves she could stay put for hours. "Sri Lanka is where almost all the precious gems can be found. Except their diamonds, of course, are nowhere as fine as the ones from South Africa. When I was down there a few years ago, I picked up a couple of emeralds. They can be set in whatever jewelry they decide."

From the kitchen came the sound of a plate shattering on the floor. Mrs. Joyce did not investigate.

"Tell him," she growled, in a manner not unlike a cow regurgitating its cud.

"Pardon me?" Zoe said.

"Are you all right, Mrs. Joyce?" Win asked.

"Tell him. Just tell him," Mrs. Joyce said. "Get it over with. Enough small talk. Otherwise—you heard him—he'll leave again and you won't ever see a dime. Off in some gin joint halfway across the world—Sri Lanka, now that's the kind of country where an irresponsible man finds happiness."

"I only visited there," Win said. "When did you last pay it a visit?"

"Don't have to go there to know."

"Hmm."

"At first I thought it was Kate," Mrs. Joyce said. "What with her reputation and all. Her mother wasn't the fine lady she is now—she had a lot of gentlemen friends. I put my money on Kate. Like mother, like daughter."

"Mrs. Joyce," Zoe said. "Please, this is not—"

"Then I thought it was Paige. Because she had always had a thing for TJ. And she was just smart enough to come up with a plan like the ones you girls cooked up. But now . . ."

Zoe saw where this was heading and stood up so abruptly that she knocked her water glass over.

"Oh, no, Mrs. Joyce, you have the wrong—"

"Winfield Skylar, don't you agree that a man would have to be an irresponsible slug . . ."

"Mrs. Joyce, stop. Please, Win, let's go."

". . . to leave a woman with his baby."

"If I had done such a thing, I couldn't agree with you more, Mrs. Joyce," Win said, rising from his seat.

"No, Mrs. Joyce, Win is not—"

Mrs. Joyce hoisted herself up from the counter. She came to the booth with surprising speed given her girth and she raised her hand to his shoulder and squeezed. Hard. Out of a reflexive gentlemanliness he sat down.

"Zoe, are we leaving?"

"Yes, absolutely."

Mrs. Joyce swung around.

"How can you go back to this man?"

"I'm not back with—"

"And him missing out on all those precious early years!"

"Well, she's still pretty young," Win said.

"I'm not talking about Zoe. She's a spinster, for crying out loud!" Mrs. Joyce glowered. Her jowly arms shook with the weight of her indignation. "She's past her sell-by date."

"Twenty-eight isn't old," Win said. "In most of the country, it's when a woman just starts to think about marriage."

"Well, this isn't most of the country," Mrs. Joyce

said. "This is Sugar Mountain we're talking about.
I've held my tongue all these years even when folks
'round here gave up trying to figure out where
Teddy came from. I figured it out long ago."

"And just who is Teddy?"

Zoe slumped into her seat muttering "no, no,
no," just as Mrs. Joyce twitched her hair so violently
that she could have slapped herself with her split
ends. She hoisted herself onto the barstool directly
in front of their booth. From beyond the door to
the kitchen they could hear the clatter of plates
and the busboy whistling a mournful country song
about being done wrong.

"Teddy is your son."

Win stared across the table.

Zoe placed her hand above her eyebrows, at the
place where a major headache was forming, almost
certainly because of the intensity of Win's gaze.

"Oh, no, Mrs. Joyce," she moaned.

"Oh, yes, Zoe. He should be told. Winfield, you
left a son behind when you went traipsing off across
the globe."

"Why, that's . . ." Win began.

Zoe closed her eyes.

"That's . . . that's . . . that's . . . that's simply
incredible."

They both knew that the word he was searching
for, the only real word that was applicable, was the
word *impossible*.

Five

"I never liked that restaurant," Win said when they hit the sidewalk. The Little Lilac screen door slammed shut; the front windowpane rattled, and Mrs. Joyce flipped the yes-we're-open sign over to its surly closed-come-again-sometime side.

Elsewhere on the planet, twilight can be an unpredictable hour; but in Sugar Mountain the few minutes before the sun takes its leave are of striking regularity. Folks get tired after punching the clock, and all they want is to go home. It's the hour when mothers fight traffic and think about the pile of laundry lurking in the basement. Kids have been told in no uncertain terms that dinner is served at six o'clock sharp and stragglers won't be fed. The post office is on Eastern Standard Time; the librarian has his kraft-paper-covered copy of a Danielle Steele on his easy chair to go home to; and Fred at the gas station is spending the summer helping his kid study for the SAT, so he closes up the minute the coast is clear.

The red lights at the corner outside the Little Lilac blinked for no one.

"Are you hungry?" Zoe asked. "I could make you a sandwich or an omelet," she said, crossing her fingers that he wouldn't say yes, because her mother would be home. "Sorry about Mrs. Joyce throwing us out."

"She didn't throw us out. She threw me out. She would have happily made you something to eat. She doesn't like me, never did. And you know what? I don't like her either."

"She has her good points."

"Name one."

Zoe looked at the car and decided on the curb-side park bench. She sat down, pulling her linen dress around her slim legs. For half a minute, she considered Mrs. Joyce.

"See?" Win said and sprawled beside her. "And while we're at it, let's talk about your mailman and his good points."

"Kurt? That's easy—he checks up on people living alone. Especially the elderly. And especially in bad weather when people can't get out of their houses."

"He sticks his nose into other people's business."

"He does do a little of that," she conceded. "All right, a lot."

"And the mayor?"

"He plans a good Fourth of July parade."

"He's pompous and self-righteous and can't hold a tune. Let's talk about the librarian."

He gestured kitty-corner to the library. The librarian had just locked the door and was adjusting the hair on top of his head which an errant breeze had brought down too low on his right sideburn.

"He's very smart."

"I don't think a man should wear hair that isn't his," Win grumbled.

"Win, you don't like Sugar Mountain."

"You're right, I don't. And I can't understand why you stay. Or why you stayed when you must have gotten so much grief for having my baby out of wedlock."

She did a double take.

"I was going to tell you. Over dinner. If it came up naturally in conversation."

"So I'm a dad."

"I haven't said that. Not to anybody. Not even Paige and Kate. And they're like sisters to me."

"But they've assumed that I am the father of your son."

"Well, yes. I suppose. No, I know they do."

"Because of that night in the Impala. No one ever believed me when I said we had fallen asleep. I guess I wouldn't have believed it either."

He regarded her speculatively.

"Really?"

"You had a reputation."

"What kind of reputation?"

"You know perfectly well what reputation. Your mother had to use a broom to sweep away all the girls holding vigil on your front porch and I'm sure your phone just about rang itself off the wall. You were dangerous with a capital D and that appeals to a certain sort of woman."

"But not your sort."

"Certainly not."

He whistled.

"Why, Zoe Kinnear. You sound almost interested in me. And here all this time I thought you were nice to me out of pity."

"It wasn't pity and I was never boy crazy," she said hotly. "I thought of you as a friend."

He leaned close.

"Never anything more?"

He said it with such a mixture of courtly jest and true emotion that any other woman would have melted, wanting more of the latter and revelling in being the subject of the former. But she was made of stronger starch.

"Absolutely not."

His breath touched the back of her neck. She felt a tiny gathering of goose bumps, normally associated with scary movies, bending too close to the freezer section at Lakeside Foods, and waking up in the middle of the night convinced she hadn't remembered to lock the door. Still, it was not unpleasant. In fact, if anything, it made her edge just the slightest bit closer to him.

"Libby thinks you and I were lovers and that I'm a hit-and-run dad."

The spell was broken. She swallowed hard.

"I'm sorry. I've let people think what they want to think. You must be terribly angry at me."

"Not at you."

"Why not?"

"Because I would have done something in that Impala if I'd been given half a chance," he said. He caught her look of disbelief. "There isn't a man who could spend the night in a car with you and not end up wanting more."

"You didn't try anything. You didn't even ask me for a kiss."

"Because you were . . . well, too nice."

She laughed.

"Too nice to kiss?"

"You had—what?—a nine-thirty curfew on weekends. And you had to wear your dresses too long—except for the cheerleading uniform. That showed off your legs real nice. Your parents didn't let you go to the homecoming parties. You taught the kindergarten Sunday school class. I couldn't kiss a girl like that—I'd change her too much, or worse, she'd change me."

"So then why did you do it yesterday? I'm still nice. I still teach kindergarten Sunday school. I don't stay out late."

"Well, you were a beautiful woman dancing by herself in the middle of the field and I've seen so much of the world that I don't think labels like nice and naughty apply to women anymore."

She pursed her lips together primly.

"Zoe, did you want me to kiss you?"

"Of course not! I told you that."

"No, I mean eleven years ago."

"Maybe," she said edgily.

"Would you have let me take your hair down?"

he asked, and reached up to take a single stray curl between his fingers.

"I don't know," she said, tugging away from him. Her fingers worked quickly to tuck the curl back into place. "Maybe."

He took her hand, turned it palm side up, and touched the pulse point of her wrist.

"Would you have let me make love to you?"

"I . . . Win, this is silly."

"There was someone else you loved. Someone who's a father."

Jerking her hand back, she stood up. Her cheeks felt hot and she was sure that when Prudence Cruikshank told her that ladies don't sweat, they glow—she had meant something like this. Her cotton-knit shell felt sticky, and she pressed her lips together.

"Sorry," he said. "Please don't go. You were a friend to me when I didn't have many friends."

She sat down, although she carefully moved an inch away from where she had been before in order to show that this was strictly friendship.

"Fred's Gas Station looks exactly the same," Win said. "Does a customer still risk getting his tobacco juice on his windshield when he's squeegeeing?"

"It's mostly self-service now," Zoe said. "But Fred fills up the tank for women."

Fred and his son emerged from the office and locked up.

"How 'bout the principal? How's she doing?"

Zoe couldn't stand the chitchat anymore.

"I'm sorry everyone thinks you're Teddy's father."

"I'm sure it surprised no one. I thought I told everybody in Sugar Mountain," Win said, amending, "everybody who would listen, that nothing, absolutely nothing, had happened in my car. That you had been trying to persuade me to go back to school and you were the first person to actually listen to why I wanted to drop out."

"Only because I had run out of reasons for you not to. Have you ever gone back to school?"

"I ask questions of people who are wise; I read books that are written to last, and I go to places where history is happening. Schools are for people who don't have the imagination to get their own education in the world."

"You sound every bit as pompous as you did when you dropped out of school."

He laughed, which is something he wouldn't have done all those years ago.

"You might be right," he said. "Because if everyone did like I did, there wouldn't be families and small towns and schools."

"That's what I told you!"

"Never thought I'd sound like you. Maybe you're one of those wise people I was talking about." He sighed. "When I leave again, will I continue to be this child's father?"

"I don't think that would be right."

"What have you told your son?"

"About his father? He doesn't ask. When he does . . . I don't know what I'll do."

"I think a child has a right to know his father. And a father . . . well, he has a right to know his child. Did you ever tell him? The father who isn't stepping up to the plate?"

She didn't say anything. A station wagon filled with girls in soccer jerseys stopped at the intersection and made a left turn. The muffler didn't work very well. A lawn mower hummed—someone trying to get the grass cut before dinner. She had maintained her silence under worse conditions.

Win sighed.

"Okay, I give up. But tell me this. Do my brothers know?"

She startled.

"Know what?"

"Know that I'm the so-called father?

"They don't know anything except that I'm the biological mom; but that's only because when they got married, each was concerned he might be Teddy's father."

Win stared.

"No, no, no!" Zoe cried. "It's not like that. I'd better explain."

"I think so."

"When I figured out I was pregnant, I went to Kate and Paige. I was very scared, especially since I'm a minister's daughter. I was supposed to be a good girl."

"Getting pregnant doesn't mean you're bad."

"In my case, it did."

"Where was I when all this was happening?"

"You were already gone when I knew I was pregnant."

He whistled.

"I thought I was doing the best thing by leaving," he said. "I would have helped you."

"The girls hatched a plan. I think it was Paige's idea at first, but maybe it was Kate's; I don't remember clearly."

"And the plan was?"

"That the three of us would be parents to Teddy. Our little boy Teddy. He wouldn't have a mom and a dad. He'd have three moms and no dad," she said, catching his doubtful gaze in the last dappling of sunlight through the trees. "It's worked far better than you'd imagine. He lives with me, spends a lot of time with Kate and Paige, and folks didn't know what to think. My mother was furious, but actually, Paige's parents weren't much happier. But once they got to see their grandchild, they were wonderful. And Matt and TJ were reassured by Kate and Paige that I was the biological mother—not them."

"Why don't you just let me talk sense into the jerk who got you pregnant? Sounds easier and more efficient than an alternative lifestyle."

"It is too late. The circumstances never . . ."

"The circumstances always warrant telling the man unless . . . he didn't hurt you, did he?"

"No, that's not it."

"Then what could possibly stop you from telling a man you've loved about the child that carries his blood, if not his name?"

They stared each other down.

"You know, I would have loved you, if you had given me a chance," Win said, turning away to regard a pickup truck full of teenagers that had stopped at the intersection. The truck roared away, leaving a cloud of exhaust. "I never knew you were involved with someone else."

"It wasn't a competition."

"If I'd known, it would have been," he concluded simply. "Your son will want to know someday."

"And I'll have to tell him. But only him. And only when he asks."

"Then what?"

"Then we'll live our lives the way we always have."

Win shook his head. He put his arm on the bench behind her shoulder, and when he got no resistance, he let it stay there.

"I can't understand why it's such a secret."

"It has to be that way."

"Zoe, I don't think you're being fair to the dad. Look at me—I'm a wanderer. I like to go places. I've been everywhere there is to be. I'm happiest when all my possessions fit into my backpack. Happiest when my passport has a lot of stamps on it. But if someone I once loved told me I have a child, I'd find me a comfortable spot and work that spot until the day I drew my last breath. I'd take care of that baby on that spot. And the mother, too."

Zoe opened her purse and shoved her hand in to look for a hankie that wasn't there.

"Aw, hell, Zoe, what's the matter?" Win asked.

"I never took you for being so conventional."

"You're right," he said. He pulled a handkerchief out of his back pocket. "Here. You're going to make *me* start crying. I never thought I'd live long enough to be a conventional human being, either."

He waited a few moments before speaking.

"How 'bout if I drive you home?"

She regarded the car warily.

"I'll walk you home. Don't worry; I won't ask to come in. I remember your mother. Ten years can't soften steel."

"She doesn't speak of you fondly," Kate said.

They both laughed. They sat for several companionable minutes until the evening breezes set in. Then they walked the four blocks to the green-gabled Kinnear house. Purple-flowered clematis had the run of a white picket fence and impatiens spilled their blooms from windowboxes.

"When are you leaving?"

"I'm finished here. I'll pack up and leave tomorrow."

"Where are you going?"

He shrugged.

"I'm based in Bhutan. I get calls from all over, from all different kinds of people. Someone will want adventure, but only if someone will hold their hand along the way. And I am a little . . . tired of Bhutan. So I might end up in Africa again. Not the settle-down sort, am I?"

"No. And I'm so settled down that it's time for me to say good night."

He took her hand and leaned forward to kiss her cheek. His lips were soft and her cheek softer still.

"Can I have a picture of him?" he asked. "Since I'm this boy's absent father, it'd be nice to have something in my wallet."

"Of course," she said. She opened her purse, and after noticing that this was the only time her keys had ever been on top of the pile of necessities, she pulled out a small cloth-bound folded picture frame. He leaned over her shoulder and she explained the two pictures. "This one is of Teddy, Kate, Paige—and that's me. It's when we first got out of the hospital."

"We?"

"Well, me and Teddy. It was in Vail, so no one knew."

"It's too dark to see very well, but what is *this* picture?"

"That's Teddy last year. He played second base in Little League. It's hard to tell in the dark." She turned the picture so that the front porch light shone on it. "But that's his team jersey. The bakery sponsored his team."

"Can I have both?"

She hesitated for only a moment.

"Yes."

They awkwardly said good night, good-bye, good luck, good life. He kissed her on the cheek and she was surprised that the feeling she had was . . . disappointment.

"Why don't you kiss me good-bye?" Her throat caught. "Really kiss me good-bye. No, really, Win.

Since you're leaving and I probably won't see you again, I don't mind telling you, you're a great kisser. And I haven't, well, I haven't had my share of kisses."

"Flattery, baby, is a wonderful thing," he said.

He took her face in his hands and, with careful, butterfly-soft kisses, erased the prim-and-properness.

"That's just for starters, darling," he said when she tugged back. He reached to take her hair out of its tight knot, but on that one point she resisted. Fine, even if he didn't get to caress the coppery silky curls, he could kiss her.

Oh, Lordy, he could kiss her.

His lips paused at her mouth, holding an electrically charged lightness between them, until she moaned, begging for more without knowing she was begging; and then he gave her everything. His tongue, his lips, even the arms with which he steadied her, they all were of one purpose.

To kiss her. Thoroughly. Completely.

Enough to last a lifetime.

When he relinquished her, she swayed against him, her eyes tightly shut. He marveled at the thick, bronze fringe of lashes that shadowed her cheeks. He counted five freckles, would have kissed every one of them just because they were cute, and traced the delicate twin angles of her upper lip.

"Oh," she said.

He chuckled.

"Do I really have to go?"

"Absolutely," she said dreamily.

"Are you gonna be all right?"

"Oh, yes," she purred. Then she opened her eyes. "Never again."

He crossed his fingers over his chest just like the Boy Scout that he never was.

"Not another kiss. Tomorrow night I'll be far away. Look at an atlas and think of me fondly."

"I always have. Oh, dear, there's Mrs. McGillicuddy hanging out her window."

"Hello, Mrs. McGilli—"

She grabbed his outstretched arm.

"Shhhh! Get going," Zoe warned. The Kinnear porch light blinked on, which was somewhat reasonable given that the sun was down and the stars were coming out to play, but not completely in keeping with routine since Mrs. Kinnear worried about the high electricity bills. "Good luck, Win, wherever you go. Send me a postcard."

"Sure. Will do."

"Must be exciting to see so many new places, all the time."

"Yeah, I guess it is exciting."

Mrs. Kinnear's face appeared at the living room window; and although Win thought it silly for any grown woman to defer to her mother so completely, he figured Zoe chose this path as the only way by which she could nurse her mother through her terminal illness.

"Good-bye, friend," he said.

He walked away from the house and did not look back until he reached the corner. And when he did, she was already inside.

Jack.

She had said *Jack*. The day before, in the mountain glade. A half-dozen not very flattering thoughts about his brother came to mind. Then he shook his head, as if to dislodge them all.

Must be another Jack. His brother had been almost twenty-five then. He would never have taken advantage of a seventeen-year-old, particularly one like Zoe, who was so sheltered and restricted. Jack would have used protection, would never have let a girl take the risk of pregnancy. And besides, hadn't Jack been dating . . . He couldn't remember clearly the weeks leading up to Jack's death. But he knew it was impossible, simply impossible that Jack had left a child behind.

Six

As Win disappeared into the next block, Mrs. Kinnear regarded her daughter. All buttons buttoned and accounted for. Hair as proper as could be. Cheeks flushed—but that was the August sun talking.

"Who was that?"

A hesitation.

"No one, Mother. Just . . . a friend."

"Where were you?"

"Just a few errands. Ran a little late. Traffic was terrible."

"There's no traffic in Sugar Mountain."

"All right, Mother," Zoe said, exasperated. "You'll hear about it sooner or later. I was with Winfield. We were going to have dinner at the Little Lilac, but . . . well, it closed early. He walked me home."

"Oh, mercy of the angels! You never learn from your mistakes, do you?"

"No, Mother," she said. "I learn too much from my mistakes."

* * *

"You saw him?" Paige asked, before delicately spooning herself a fourth helping of Zoe's rice pudding. Although she was barely six weeks pregnant, she ate for two. Or maybe three.

Zoe nodded.

"Was his hair still long?" Matt asked. Zoe considered Win's hair and opened her mouth to reply, but before she could, the sheriff of Sugar Mountain had a few other questions about his long-lost brother. "And did he get another tattoo? Does he still smoke? Drink? Did he say anything about keeping on the right side of the law? I hope he wasn't drag racing on my streets."

"He only did that a few times in high—" Zoe began.

"Did he say what he'd been doing for the past ten years?" TJ demanded. "For instance, finishing school? Getting a job? Being a little responsible?"

"Uh, well, actually, he has a job as—"

"Why did he leave again?" Kate asked. "Why couldn't he stay just for dinner tonight?"

Paige, TJ, Matt, and Kate had other questions, too. Each one was more important than the one before. Their questions came fast and furious. But none of them got answered.

"Enough!" Paige cried out, throwing her spoon down onto her empty dessert bowl. "Maybe we should let Zoe answer one question before asking her another."

"Oh, no," Zoe said, patting her lips with her napkin. "It's much more fun to listen to you four interrupt each other."

That quieted the two couples.

"Zoe, you just let us blather on about mundane little matters," Kate said, "when you were sitting on the most important news of all."

"But I like your news."

The day after she had said goodbye to Win, Zoe was invited to Paige and TJ's new home for a dinner to welcome back the newlyweds, Matt and Kate.

Zoe had squelched yawns during Paige's account of new banking regulations that she had learned of during her recent trip to New York. Since she was president of Sugar Mountain's only bank, it was important for Paige to know these arcane ways with money. Zoe had also oohed and aaahed with just the right amount of enthusiasm over TJ's selections from a New York baby boutique where he had spent much of his time while his wife was in meetings.

Zoe had, with equal parts patience and quiet enthusiasm, listened to Matt and Kate's account of their honeymoon in California, from which they had just returned a few hours before. Photos were passed around over a fresh green bean and tomato salad Paige had concocted in the kitchen. You-look-like-you-were-having-fun's accompanied the potato salad Kate had brought. The two brothers were given the praise they were due—and then some—for the ribs they grilled on the porch.

But full stomachs sometimes make for melancholy reflection, and Zoe's rice pudding was an especially thoughtful dish. It was then that TJ sighed heavily and told the gathering that Win had come into town, but it was just on business.

"I left a message at the Sports Shop saying we'd love to have him here for dinner this evening. The manager said he hadn't seen him all day."

"Just like Win—probably off climbing or hiking and is going to come home just when everyone is worried sick."

It was only then that Zoe mentioned that Win had left town already—this time for good.

"Why'd he have to leave town before any of us got a chance to see him?" TJ asked as his wife slid his bowl away from him.

"He has a place in Bhutan."

TJ stared at her. He was part of the ninety-nine and three-quarters percent of the Sugar Mountain population that thought there was more to that night in the Impala. But he was too much of a gentleman to have ever said a word. And he was too good a brother to have ever believed Win was Teddy's father. Because Win would never have abandoned Zoe . . . or would he?

"He looks the same," Zoe added. She wasn't used to the attention, to her friends and their husbands staring at her with such open-mouthed concentration. "He's exactly the same, just older. The tattoo—I think it's the same one, the Sacred Heart. On his shoulder. He was wearing a thin shirt and I think I saw the outline of it."

Matt nodded.

"And his hair is long, down around his shoulders."

Kate nodded.

"He says he gets lots of calls from people who want guides, especially in the Himalayas. It's very popular to take vacations that have a little more to them than sitting by a hotel pool."

"Hey, sitting by the pool was good enough for us," Kate said amiably. "We had a wonderful honeymoon, didn't we, darling?"

Matt nodded.

TJ clenched his jaw. Paige reached out to pat his hand. "Why are you upset?"

TJ shook his head.

"Each of us had a share in the shop after Dad died."

"What does that have to do with his visit?" Paige asked.

"He cashed out his share."

"Oh, no," Paige said.

"Will the store survive?" Kate asked.

"We've reinvested so often that it's doing quite well," TJ conceded. "But I don't know why he needs so much cash all of a sudden."

"Gambling," Matt said. "He liked to play cards. He said poker was just a matter of memorizing the cards that had been shown and calculating probabilities of cards still in the deck. He could do it all in his head, but maybe he hit a bad patch."

"He'd be paying off a lot of cards," TJ said.

He mentioned a figure that was substantial

enough to quiet the dining room for several moments.

"Did he say what he needed the money for?" Paige asked Zoe.

"No, we didn't talk about that."

"*Well,* did you . . . you know, tell him about Teddy?"

"I gave him his picture. That's about it."

There was quiet. Absolute quiet.

"Am I to assume that Win is Teddy's—?" Matt asked. He might have said more, but a sudden grunt indicated a wifely kick under the table.

"I told you when we got married that we are all three his mother."

"But Win isn't taking responsibility—"

"We don't know that he's . . ."

"I thought we agreed that we would never ask Zoe to say . . ."

"It's possible Win is Teddy's father," TJ said. "In which case he should be told."

"QUIET!"

For the second time in the evening, Zoe brought the room to heel. Uncomfortable with her friends and their husbands for the first time in her life, she rose to her feet and picked up the rice pudding serving dish.

"I think it would be best if we just said good night," Zoe said.

Paige shot her husband a don't-you-feel-like-a-heel-now? look. TJ hung his head. Kate stood up and held her hands out to Zoe for a hug, but Zoe shook her head.

"When Teddy comes home from camp, I'm going to have to explain to him about his father. But until then, I intend to keep my mouth shut and I would hope you would, too."

"Are we to assume . . ." TJ said.

"You may assume nothing."

She charged out of the dining room with Kate and Paige hot on her heels. TJ and Matt were so shell-shocked that their apologies came out choked and stumbling.

Zoe turned to her friends only when she reached the foyer.

"The idea of protecting my reputation by giving Teddy three moms worked only as long as we all stayed exactly as we were, single and alone, pining away for men who were unattainable. But now it's not working."

"But you are our family," Kate mewed.

"And Win was trouble, through and through," Paige added. "He ran out on you when you needed him most."

Zoe shook her head, opened the front door, and stepped out into the cool summer night. The fireflies and mosquitoes danced about in the darkness. Unsure of her footing, she reached back into the foyer and flicked on the porch light. In doing so, she illuminated a figure walking up the steps.

"Hey," Win said, holding aloft three bouquets of fresh white roses. "Am I late for dinner?"

Kate shouldered out from behind Zoe and stood in front of Win, rebuffing his offer of flowers.

"What are you doing here?"

"I finally got somebody to give me directions. Nice house, Paige."

"Do you know you have a son?" Kate blurted out.

"Good evening to you, too."

She growled with animalistic fury, looked as if she might use her raised hand to slap him, and then was punctured as surely as a balloon when he said "You're right, Kate; you're absolutely right. I'm a dad. Ain't it grand?"

"Win, you're playing with fire," Zoe said and then shook her head. "Good night."

She charged down the street, enveloped in the sleeping town's darkness.

"I gotta run. One of these is for Paige. By the way, welcome to the Skylar family, both of you," Win said, shoving two bouquets of flowers into Kate's hands while reserving the finest and fullest bouquet to give to Zoe.

Paige and Kate stood on the front porch, staring down the street, long after Zoe and Win had turned the corner.

Zoe was halfway down the next block when he caught up with her.

"I brought you flowers," he said.

She neither turned to regard the beautiful bouquet nor broke her stride to acknowledge his presence.

"I brought them flowers, too, but they don't seem too thankful."

"I thought you were leaving," she complained in a most un-Zoe-like manner.

"I spent too long looking at the photograph."

That stopped her in her tracks. She whirled to face him.

He held out the flowers as if to suggest that only by having this burden taken from him could he locate the photograph. Or maybe like a man holding a shield. She did not take the flowers.

He shrugged, held the flowers in one hand, and reached with the other into the back pocket of his khakis.

"Here," he said, pointing to the picture of Teddy in his Little League uniform. "You and my son."

Slowly, not giving anything in the way of encouragement, she leaned over the rim of her dish and regarded the photograph. She reared up her shoulders.

"So?"

"You're not looking very close."

"Win, you and I are the only people on the planet who know with one-hundred-percent certainty that you are not the father of this child."

He smiled loopily.

"Funny how knowledge works, isn't it? We're the only people who know exactly what happened in that car, and yet there isn't a Sugar Mountain resident who doesn't think there was a healthy dose of hanky-panky. And how many think I'm a dad?"

"I would say Sugar Mountain residents are about evenly divided on those who think Kate, Paige, or me the mom."

"But it's not going to stay like that with those two married. Reality often gets in the way of our best laid plans."

"You're right. Our arrangement has already been destroyed," Zoe admitted ruefully. "We'll have to talk to Teddy when he comes back from camp. We'll tell him that I'm his biological mother but that Kate and Paige love him every bit as much. We—meaning Kate, Paige, and I."

"And about his father?"

They stared at each other for a long moment before Zoe felt the tears welling in her eyes.

"It was Jack, wasn't it?"

She opened her mouth. Started to speak. Thought better of it.

"Tell me the truth," Win said.

"Yes," she said, sighing heavily. "I've always wondered how people can look at Teddy and not see Jack. I see Jack every time I look at my boy."

"He's got a lot of you, too."

Zoe's head drooped. She felt suddenly a great weariness, the weariness of someone who has tried for so many years to maintain a cheerful face and a dead man's reputation.

"He's mostly Jack," she said and then remembered herself. Win brought her chin up to a challenging angle. "I'm not talking to anyone but Teddy—and only when he asks. So you can't say a word."

He bowed his head ever so slightly in acquiescence to her maternal right.

"Are you going to swear him to secrecy?"

She closed her eyes and chose her next words very carefully.

"I'm going to tell him that I think it would hurt certain people very much if he were to be open about it. Jack's been dead for a long time."

"If your goal is to keep Jack's name out of this, it won't take long for folks to pry it out of your son. He'd have to be a mighty strong person not to talk—to Kate, to Paige, to one of my brothers. Lot of pressure on a boy."

"I have been thinking about that," she conceded.

"Now if it were me, I'd just let it rip. I'm the kind that would just tell everyone the truth and hurt feelings be damned. But you've been protecting Jack's reputation for a long time. Tough habit to break."

"I'll manage."

She murmured good night and, with stately grace, walked the sidewalk to her home.

"I'd like to marry you," he called after her. "Make an honest woman of you."

She paused only a moment, the barest trembling—it could have just been the breeze—her only reaction.

"I'm already honest."

"I'd just be doing the right thing," he added. "Better late than never. Finally taking responsibility. Being a good citizen and a good father."

"You're not talking about staying in Sugar Mountain, are you?" she asked, over her shoulder.

"No, but if I married you, folks would assume . . ."

"That you were just trying to do the right thing," she said. Turning. Intrigued.

"And then when I left . . ."

"That you were just giving in to your nature."

"And then nobody asks Teddy anything . . ."

"And everyone believes what they want to believe."

"About Jack."

"About Jack."

He pressed his advantage, taking two broad steps forward but carefully not crowding her. A delicate negotiation required a delicate touch.

"We'd still be the only two people on earth who knew what happened in that car. Well, I guess three, if you want your talk with Teddy to be that detailed. But it would take all that pressure off your shoulders. You wouldn't be a single mother—no, no, you'd be a wife who happens to be married to a rat. And in this small town, I think that's a step up."

She stood for several minutes. Then shook her head.

"Thank you for the proposal, if that's what that was."

"It was."

"When I marry, I'll marry for love. I've waited all these years for love. I'm willing to wait a little longer. But you're sweet to ask."

He was momentarily stymied when she refused. But then he ran the three short steps to catch up with her and shoved the flowers through her arm so that she was forced to accept them or risk dropping her dish.

"I know you don't love me," he said. "But it could still work. It would be a marriage of convenience, as they call these things."

"I don't know who THEY are, but THEY take marriage too lightly."

They approached the small cottage with white siding and pale lilac shutters. He held open the gate for her.

"What if I said I loved you?" he asked conversationally.

"Win, don't be silly. You haven't seen or spoken to me in eleven years. You don't even know who I am anymore."

"I love the most important things about you. I love your red hair, high moral standards, the way your lips get thin when you're mad—and you have great legs, too. But most of all, I love kissing you. I've only done it twice, but I think I could get used to doing it more."

She shook her head with the same weariness as when Teddy professed not to understand why dinner came before dessert, bedtime was bedtime, and homework was more important than video games.

"Then you'd have to live in Sugar Mountain, because I don't marry for convenience, I marry for love. And to be in love with me, you'd have to love every person in this town, because they are a part of me. You'd have to love being here, even when it's more fun to be somewhere else. You'd have to love the sameness, the routine, even the boredom—

because that's what a small town has to offer. You'd have to love the fact that I love this town. And you'd have to love me even if I'm a goody-two-shoes and would never wear a red dress. You'd have to love the fact that I go to church every Sunday and don't drive a mile over the speed limit and never keep a book out of the library past its due date. You'd have to love my mother, who will always be the most vigorous invalid in the state. And most of all, Win, you'd have to love me not just because Jack died and left me with his baby but because of who I am."

His shoulders slumped.

"That's a lot. But what if I could?"

"Don't put yourself through that for my sake. I'll figure out what to tell my son. And I've learned to not tell anyone in this town anything I wouldn't want posted on the announcement board outside the high school. Thank you for your offer. I can manage, Win."

Wordlessly, she asked him to hold her dish and the flowers while she got her keys out from her purse.

"Can I ask you one thing?"

"Sure."

"Would you have given me a chance to love you?"

"In high school?"

"When you were in high school, yes."

She shook her head.

"You were too wild. Jack is the right man for me."

"You're using the present tense."
She shoved her key in the lock and turned.
"I know."
"But he's gone."
She opened the door.
"Don't think I haven't figured that out."
And with that, she said a crisp good night.

Seven

The next morning, Zoe ate her puffed rice over the kitchen sink. Did not linger over the television as she washed the dishes—most definitely did not let herself flip the channel to the Jerry Springer reruns or the newest Oprah, because either of those might cause her mind to wander. And wandering was not good.

She dressed quickly, choosing a sensible beige rayon shift with a matching short-sleeve jacket. She put her hair up into a bun so tight her eyes had an exotic almond shape until she let her hair down and pulled it back up, this time a little, but not much, looser. When she ran into the librarian as he began his day, she clipped the word *hello* so frostily that she just as easily could have been blowing ice crystals onto the tips of his toupee, though it was pushing ninety-five degrees in the shade of the beech trees.

She registered forty children for Sunday school, accepting the forms and the nominal checks from mothers with a rare businesslike attitude and a sharp retort for anyone who said that they were too busy to volunteer to teach this year.

When Faye Barron, who lived across the street, mentioned that she had returned to her pantry just the night before with a hankering for the last piece of a key lime pie and that when she ate said pie beside the living room bay window she noticed that the Kinnear porch light was turned on and that on investigating further by leaning out her window she noticed that a gentleman (long hair, disreputable looking) left by the front gate and . . . Zoe fixed on her a gaze so blankly innocent that Faye was forced to conclude that she had been mistaken, that perhaps it was another house, perhaps there had been no gentleman caller, and perhaps she just would write out her check, turn in her form, and ask that her little Glynna be put in the same class as her best friend Alice.

"We don't accept friendship requests," Zoe said, adding pointedly, "This is a small enough town that everyone should and can be friends with everyone else."

Faye Barron agreed, *oh, yes, of course, we're all very good friends, I never for a moment meant to imply otherwise*, and backed out of the office quickly. Zoe knew that, as in every year, she would assign Glynna to the same class as Alice. And that Faye would bring snacks every Sunday for the kids. And that Faye always hung out of her window to catch the view of her neighbors' homes.

Just as surely as she knew that she would call Faye later and apologize for being in a sour mood—she would blame it on summer allergies, the full moon, or the excessive heat. Faye would accept the apology graciously—allergies were reported to be worse than usual, the full moon did make people go crazy, and the heat was just enough to make a woman scream.

Neither woman would mention the true cause of Zoe's distress.

It was not that Zoe intended to be cold or distant or abrupt. It was not that Zoe wanted to purse her lips together in a tight, prim line. It was not that she wanted to sound prissy when she told the reverend that he needed to include an encouragement for volunteers to teach Sunday school in his next sermon because if he didn't there wouldn't be anybody to do it. It was not that she liked the way her foot tapped impatiently when Mrs. Nielson hemmed and hawed over whether she could help with the rummage sale. It was not that she liked herself, not one little bit, when Peggy Martin told her that her son was gifted, really bright, and should be placed in the class two grades ahead of himself and Zoe said, "Look, everybody's above average these days."

Zoe knew she had turned, overnight, into something approximating a Cruikshank sister—and she was not a member of the Cruikshank family. After eating her chicken salad at the Little Lilac counter—staring down Mrs. Joyce with uncharacteristic boldness that made the restaurateur's ponytail bob up and down—Zoe decided that she needed sunblock.

Or road salt.

Or birdseed. It was never too early to stock up for winter.

The bells of the Skylar Sports Shop rang cheerily when she entered. The manager grunted hello and put his *Detour* magazine under the counter.

"Help you, Miss Zoe?"

"Uh, yes, I'm looking for . . . um . . ." She glanced around. Her eyes came to rest on a selection of skateboards. "Skateboards?"

The manager muttered something that could have been interpreted as "gimme a break."

"He's upstairs," he said, shoving a plug of chewing tobacco between his cheek and gum.

"I never said . . ."

The tobacco plug distorted his face and voice.

"I know. But not saying don't make him downstairs, now, does it?"

"Well, I never!"

"Don't ever say *never*, Miss Zoe. You don't know what you'll feel like tomorrow."

She marched purposefully up to the second-floor apartment. In the doorway to a small bedroom, she paused, catching her breath. He was packing his backpack. There wasn't much to show for his being in his thirties. A few books, a Bible (this surprised her), some clothes, a photograph album, and a camera.

He glanced up. He hadn't shaved and his eyes looked weary.

"I just came to say good-bye," she said. "I thought you should know I appreciate your offer.

But of course, it's really quite impossible. It means a lot to me that you would care enough about me to want to make an honest woman of me."

"But you already are one," he grunted. "Crazy of me to ask you like that. Better to be unmarried than to be—"

"It's not you."

He didn't answer, which was just the same as answering "like hell."

"Did anyone while you were here tell you the story of Rory Packer?"

"You mean the Rory a few years ahead of us in school—the photography club guy?"

"Yes," she said, using the opportunity to slip beyond him and sit down on a chair by the bureau. "He did everyone's weddings, christenings, portraits, did all the class photographs for the school. He's a tenor."

Win scowled.

"In the church choir. Used to be, at least. Now we don't have a tenor. But I'm getting ahead of myself."

"Okay, so you lost a tenor."

"I became friendly with him."

Win sat on the bed, not quite turning to look at her, wearily resigning himself to hearing the story.

"How friendly?"

"Friendly enough. We went out for four years. This was after Teddy had started nursery school. We went out every Friday night to the Little Lilac with Teddy. We sometimes went to the movies. In

Breckenridge, with Teddy, of course. They both liked the animated Disney movies."

"Zoe, does this have a point? Because I'm getting ready to clear out. I have a plane to catch. I missed one yesterday thinking I could solve a problem for a friend."

"The point is that we were a couple for four years."

"That's a long time."

"Very. He started asking me to marry him after, oh, six months."

"And I bet you said no."

"Correct."

"Did you tell him that you were in love with Jack?"

"I couldn't do that because then he'd have known that Jack was Teddy's father."

"Did you tell him you were in love with me? Would have been mighty convenient, what with me gone."

"No, I didn't say anything about being in love with anybody. I just said I wasn't ready. Because I really thought it was just a matter of being ready, of letting go, of saying good-bye to Jack in my heart."

"So, how many times did Rory ask you?"

She swallowed hard at the painful memory.

"About once a month."

"For three-and-a-half years?"

She sat down next to him on the bed. Her shoulders slumped in an uncharacteristic show of poor posture.

"Yes."

"Jeeez. Got to hand it to Rory. That's persistence."

"It gets worse."

"Okay, I'll bite."

"I woke up one morning and opened my Sugar Mountain *Chronicle*. I read the front pages and the mayor's column; I think it was something about zoning for multi-family dwellings. Of course, there're not enough folks in Sugar Mountain to—"

"Get to the point!"

She worried the hem of her skirt before blurting it out.

"I turned to the announcements page and saw my engagement to Rory. With a picture of the two of us and everything."

"Oh, boy. That was the first you heard about it?"

She nodded miserably.

"I broke it off immediately. Called the paper—they were wonderful and printed a retraction the next day—and as gently as I could, I told Rory I couldn't marry him."

"Because of Jack."

"I didn't tell him because of Jack. But it was because of Jack."

"And now Sugar Mountain doesn't have a decent photographer and the choir doesn't have a tenor."

"Exactly. He cleared out the next day. Went out East. His mother was furious with me. She blames me for not having her son around."

"Understandable."

"And so I want you to know it's not you."

"Well, we won't have to worry about Sugar Mountain's losses because you've refused my proposal," Win said, standing up. He heaved his backpack up on his shoulder. "All this town'll be missing is, well, nothing but a tenor and me."

"No, Win, it's not like that. People love you."

"I have to go."

"You don't even know where you're going. You don't have a home."

"That's not the point. I like to go anywhere. I told you last night, there's nothing finer than a backpack and no particular destination."

He paused at the screen door leading to the fire escape. He looked back at the bed.

"You know, Zoe, you have to look at reality. He's dead. Let go of him. I had to; you can, too."

She nodded. She knew. How well she knew.

"After he died, I only wished for two things. To be a good mother and to be a good daughter."

"You should have asked for three," Win said, and touching her cheek with just the tip of his index finger, he walked out.

A week ago, when he had returned stateside, he'd bought a small red BMW convertible at a San Diego "gently owned" dealership near the airport, startling the owner by paying cash and not quibbling over price. He intended to leave the car in Sugar Mountain as a peace offering to his brother Matt, whom he was sure was still living there. He hadn't expected TJ would be around—he figured

TJ for out East, New York or whatnot, making a lot of money.

At the time he had felt a nostalgic joy in the tomato red of the car, remembering the sweet-faced minister's daughter who had tried to talk him out of leaving school, tried to talk him out of smoking cigarettes, tried to talk him out of—well, just about everything until she got plum tired out. Girls who weren't used to late bedtimes should not stay up late in his car. He had intended on waking her up, intended on driving her home. Instead, as she slept, he pointed out the stars to her, naming every constellation, recounting the myths of each, explaining some of the recent advances in astrophysics. Until he, too, had fallen asleep, her scent of lilies of the valley and Ivory soap his last lullaby. All this was encompassed in every red car he had ever spotted, whether on a crowded European boulevard or a muddy African bush route.

She had never said a word about his brother Jack that night.

Now, in the alley outside the Skylar Sports Shop, he thought the car too flashy. A solid SUV or a pickup truck would have been more practical. Renting would have been cheaper, not that cheaper mattered. Matt wouldn't need this car, wouldn't want this car, and frankly, giving his brother a red car seemed to be cheapening his own recollections.

He stuck the key in the passenger-side door lock. Turned. Nothing happened. One thing about this car was bad locks. He tried several times, gave up, walked around to the driver-side door, and tried that.

The door popped open with a shudder that seemed to say "Hey, I was going to open up when I felt like it." He shoved the backpack in the sliver of room behind the front seat. He threw the dress, gaudy and unwanted, on the passenger seat. It had seemed like a good idea at the time to give it to her.

He glanced sourly around the alley. He didn't mind leaving. He almost wished there were a dog to kick, not that he'd ever kicked a dog or would ever want to kick a dog, but he did feel the need to do something to express his feelings.

So he snipped a petunia blossom off the fire escape window box and crushed it beneath his feet. He felt immediately guilty, touched as he had been in the past decade by the teachings of the Eastern mystics who prayed on the highest Himalayan slopes.

"Forgive me, Petunia," he said, but his words didn't carry the natural grace of the Nepalese or Tibetans because he was what he was. An American. A man of action. A simple guy with simple tastes—until, unfortunately, he had developed a taste for a woman he had always considered unattainable.

He got in the car, turned the ignition, and roared out onto Chestnut Avenue. But instead of turning left, onto the well-traveled street leading to the highway, he turned right, heading straight into the mountains.

The Misses Prudence and Emmeline Cruikshank stood at the mouth of the alley, both on tiptoes, both holding their hands to hats that long, bejeweled hat pins had failed to hold against the plumes of smoke, dust, and exhaust left in the wake of the sinfully red car.

"My heavens!" Emmeline exclaimed. "Doesn't that baby look hot! That's a car and a man who could fire up my engines."

"Emmeline, you talk as if you admire such reckless driving. That man, Winfield Skylar, did not come to a full and complete stop at the intersection."

"There was no one around."

"There was us! We could have been run over!"

At just that moment, before they ventured across the alley on the off-chance that a second fiery red car might speed along, the sisters observed Zoe alighting the from fire escape stairs at the side of the Sports Shop.

"Zoe, you'll never believe what just happened!" Prudence said.

"You saw Win."

"Yes and he didn't come to a full and . . ." Prudence gasped. "Was he . . . with you?"

Zoe nodded.

"In that case, I've come to a very important decision," Prudence said. And her impeccable posture became even more impeccable. "I will renew my term as president of the Women's Service Board. You can't possibly be entrusted with such a responsibility. Moral turpitude and all. Come along, Emmeline."

And as she drew herself up to her regal five feet,

two inches, Prudence instructed her sister to follow her path with a sharp jolt of her head. Emmeline said good day to Zoe, and as she followed her sister, turned only once to give Zoe a thumb's-up.

"He's got a nice, tight butt," she mouthed.

"He's leaving, you know," Zoe called out. "Gone for good."

"Exactly so," Prudence said, without breaking stride.

The back route to the mountain was not difficult, three-quarters of it could be taken by automobile, and when Win parked and changed into his hiking boots, he reached the peak in less than an hour. Without breaking a sweat.

It was always easier in summer.

The accident had been just before Christmas. TJ was home from college; Matt had dug his head out of the books; Jack had just given the pink slip to a pretty little ski bunny out of Vail—Win searched his memory and now wondered whether she was before, after, or even during the romance he'd conducted with Zoe. He'd give his brother the benefit of the doubt—ski bunny before, Zoe after.

Win was no stranger to how adventurers, climbers, tourists, even the natural sprawl of hundred-year-old communities, could leave a mark on the unspoiled beauty of of nature. There are empty water bottles on the lower slopes of Everest, candy wrappers floating in the Amazon, abandoned ranch houses in the African velds. But he thought the area where his brother had lost his footing, his rope, and ultimately his life, was largely as it had been more than a decade before. The last time he had stood here, hundreds of white and blue ribbons and bouquets of flowers had been thrown down the craggy face of the mountain. They had since been swept away by Mother Nature.

He sat down, took a swig from a bottle of water stored in the car, and composed himself.

Eleven years ago, he and Jack had taken TJ and Matt up the slope. TJ was in college out East. Matt was still in high school. Jack was making money, lots of money, guiding tourists up and down the Vail-area peaks with Win, always making sure the stragglers didn't get left behind. Treadmill tourists, the sort that work out twice a week at a cushy health club and expect an adventure vacation to take them beyond their limits—but not too far. And they wanted danger—but not too much.

That December weekend the weather didn't cooperate. A group of stockbrokers pulled out at the last minute. Jack was mildly upset about missing out on the money, but he quickly made other arrangements.

"Let's take TJ and Matt up," he told Win as they drove back to Sugar Mountain.

The two younger boys were out of school for Christmas break. Out of practice, definitely. Out of shape, never. Scared off by the weather, absolutely not.

They should have been. Within two hours of leav-

ing home, Jack was dead, his body crushed from a
fall off the razor-sharp face of the mountain.

Win had never talked to a ghost. Never talked to
an angel or an apparition. Wasn't particularly spiri-
tual. When he was invited to the sky burial of a
Sherpa he had hired, he didn't feel his friend in
the breeze as the monks insisted he would. Win
didn't pray, at least, not with any regularity—and
try as he might, he couldn't remember much more
than the Lord's Prayer and only the beginning of
the Twenty-third Psalm. He didn't even talk to himself, even in the loneliest of circumstances. But still,
he cleared his throat.

"Jack, she's put her life on hold for ten years.
Had your son—alone. Hasn't asked for much, just
two wishes—to be a good mother and to be a good
daughter. Let go of her."

Although Win had always had his share of girls,
it was always Jack they'd wanted—first. Funny that
it had been that way with Zoe, too. He had always
thought her immune to Jack's charming ways.

"Let go of her," he repeated.

Nothing about the mountain changed. The star-
pitch sparrows fought in the trees. A black-tailed
squirrel dashed through the fern leaves. A mosquito alighted on his forehead and he waved it
away.

"All right, I'm leaving," he shouted.

It was a dry, hot August. And the conifers threw
off their weakest needles in an effort to conserve
their strength for deepening root structure. So

when Win's boot came down on the path, there was the faintest snapping of camel-colored needles.

"I can't go until I know she's loved."

Win stopped, eyeballing the terrain.

"What?"

Nothing.

Hallucinating, that's what he was doing. All this talk about Jack was making him crazy. He glanced at his watch. A three-hour drive to the airport. He had to leave now.

"I can't go until I know she's loved. Really loved."

He studied the foliage carefully. Nothing. Unless Mr. Squirrel was linguistically talented, he was hearing things.

"Jack, I'm not the guy for the job," he shouted. "Because I could never stay here. So why don't you get Rory back?"

And he walked down the trail to where he had left the car. He did not look back. And though he waited and even hoped, he didn't hear much more than the sparrows fighting in the trees and the click-click-click of the locusts.

Eight

"You must have slugs, huh?" Mimi Perkins said, throwing the carton of Camels on the counter. "Cigarettes are the best, but it takes so much patience. Have you ever thought of using eggshells?"

"Eggshells?" Zoe asked absently, looking up from her perusal of the kraft paper-covered magazines displayed behind the counter of the Stop'N'Shop. "What do you use the eggshells for?"

Mimi leaned forward, exposing an expanse of bosom and the slightest hint of Tabu.

"You crush them," she said confidentially. "And then you lift up the leaves of the hostas and put a ring of crushed eggshells all around the root ball. When the slugs come out of the dirt at night and try their little slither up the hosta stem, the eggshells cut them to pieces." She made a slicing motion not unlike the chef in the Ginzu knife commercial. "Next morning, you can see the residue glistening in the mud. Looks like hair gel. With eggshells in it."

"Eeeuw."

"I like it better than the cigarette method because I don't have time to sit out in the garden all night burning slugs with cigarettes."

"Mimi, I don't have slugs."

"Really?"

"I'm going to smoke these," Zoe said, nudging the Camel carton.

Mimi's face widened in horror and then a twinkle appeared behind her thick, tortoise-framed glasses. She laughed.

"Oh, Zoe, you kidder," she said. She eyed the six-pack of wine coolers that Zoe had placed next to the cigarette carton. "Anyhow, it's not wine coolers you need; you need beer. You pour the beer into empty cat-food cans. You must have lots of those, your mother having so many cats."

"Three."

"Well, still, three cats is three too many," Mimi said, ringing up the purchases. "I'm a dog person myself. Anyhow, you dig a hole for the can right up next to the root ball of the hosta and pour a little inch of beer in it and then the slugs will—"

"I don't have slugs," Zoe repeated. "I'm drinking the wine coolers. I'm smoking the cigarettes. And I'd like that *Cosmopolitan* magazine. It looks interesting."

Mimi clamped her lips together in a tight, disapproving line and slid the month's issue of *Cosmopolitan* across the counter. The cover model showed no more cleavage than the usual *Cosmo* cover model—and in fact, her come-here-you-tiger-you look was less lascivious than the previous month's

or the month before that. The featured article—
"Sex Tricks To Drive Him Wild"—was simply standard *Cosmo* fare. In fact, Mimi could have told Zoe
that the article rehashed the naughty bits found in
the "Sexual Secrets of a Hollywood Madam" (June
issue). Black or red underwear, telling him how
much he turns you on, raking your fingernails
along his back, playing Barry White albums, etc.,
etc., etc.

"Does this have anything to do with a certain
somebody moving into town?" Mimi asked, punching numbers on the keypad of the cash register
with the pads of her fingers so as not to break her
acrylic tips.

"If you're talking about Winfield, he's already
left," Zoe said. Though she was not inclined toward
gossip, she felt gossip could be nipped in the bud
as soon as the information about Win's leaving
passed through the proper channels. And what better and more proper channel than Mimi?

But then she remembered that Mimi was also the
person from whom she was purchasing items she
had never, not once, tried before.

"So, what's with this stuff?" Mimi asked. "That'll
be $14.12, by the way. I mean, you come into this
store every week since we opened. You buy bottled
water, *Time* magazine, and when you're feeling especially daring, you buy a Twinkie or a Ho-Ho. And
Teddy buys Slurpies and if he spills, he cleans up
after himself, which I appreciate since most of the
men in this town are slobs."

Zoe counted out two fives and five ones. She

didn't dare tell Mimi that this was the modern day equivalent of an exorcism.

"You are the church secretary," Mimi added. "A minister's daughter. You're the chairman of the blood drive and PTA president."

She listed four or five other volunteer endeavors of which Zoe was the chairwoman, board member, or general all-around good-deed-doer.

"Mimi, what's so wrong with my buying cigarettes, wine coolers, and a magazine on a Saturday afternoon? Other women do it all the time or you wouldn't make enough money to keep this store open."

"But that's what I'm trying to say—you're not like other women!"

Mimi gaped, as startled by her words as Zoe was. And yet, once said, there was no doubting the wisdom and truth she spoke. Zoe was different.

"Mimi, how old do you think I am?"

"Easy. You're turning twenty-nine. We were in the same grade. You got the A's."

"And you've done a lot of living since school."

"Oh, yeah." Mimi shrugged. "A few years as a ski-bunny at Vail, went to New York, came back home when I found out I was too big-boned to be a supermodel, married Jim, bought this store, had two kids and . . ."

"But you're happy now."

"Sure, I guess. Wouldn't mind winning the lottery. But I guess I'm pretty content. Had an awful lot of growing up to do. If I hadn't seen with my own eyes just how many mistakes people can make with their lives . . ." She sized up Zoe. "I always thought folks made too big of a deal about you and Win. There were plenty of girls who put out in their boyfriends' cars. Me, included. But we're moms now, too old for that kind of stuff. I can't keep my eyes open past ten o'clock and I don't buy jeans to make my butt look good; I buy 'em to last."

Zoe looked at the Cosmopolitan cover model. Her hair was billowy; her breasts came together in a long, dark line, and her dress was the color of Campbell's tomato soup.

"Mimi, what would you think of a red dress?"

Mimi took out a paper bag and flipped it open. "Red makes my acne look more prominent."

"No. On me."

"You, in a red dress? I guess it'd be okay 'cept for your hair. I've always heard redheads . . . oh, no, you're talking about that dress Win sent you. Kurt came in here the other morning, and from the sound of it, you would have thought the thing had been shipped direct from Frederick's of Hollywood."

"It was really quite beautiful."

"Oh, Zoe, you are having a real midlife crisis. Just a couple of decades early."

She reached under the counter to produce a Twinkie and a copy of *Playgirl* wrapped in kraft paper, both of which she shoved into the paper bag with the rest Zoe's purchases.

"But it's like Judy Garland said, Zoe. There's no place like home. And for you, home isn't a place—it's your way of doing business," she said. She added in a loud, brassy voice as Mrs. McGillicuddy approached the cash register with a TV dinner and a *Soap Opera Digest,* "That's right, Zoe, cigarettes will get rid of those slugs right quick."

"I've always used eggshells," Mrs. McGillicuddy said, nodding a greeting to Zoe. "Slugs destroyed my hostas last year. You poor girl, I hope you get rid of them. But at least you don't have deer thinking your flower bed's a salad bar. Like I do."

Zoe thanked Mimi and Mrs. McGillicuddy for their concern and left the store.

"We don't smoke," her mother declared.

"I know; I was just going to try one. And if I don't like it, I'll use it to kill the slugs."

Mrs. Kinnear crossed her arms over her chest. Zoe pulled the issue of *Cosmo* out of the bag. Her mother grunted. She placed the *Playgirl* on top of the *Cosmo,* face down, but her mother turned it over. Her displeasure was registered with a sigh meant to convey hope that this was just a phase—preferably one that would be over by dinner time. But when Zoe took the six-pack of wine coolers and put it on the kitchen counter, her mother could not help but speak out.

"We do not drink," she said. "The church does not allow it."

"That was fifty years ago."

"We still—"

"Mom, I'm not talking about dancing naked through the house drinking, smoking, and—"

"Oh, stop!" her mother said, putting her hands over her ears. "Zoe you are being such a trial to me!"

The two women stared at each other.

"Mother, I have done my best to live up to your standards, to do what is right over what is pleasurable or fun, to give more than I receive, to ask what I can do for my community instead of what's in it for me. I have only tried to do two things—be a good mother and a good daughter. And if you think I've failed at my two tasks in life, then I'm sorry."

It was the longest uninterrupted speech that Zoe had ever made. It shocked both of them.

"What are you trying to do?" her mother asked.

"Consider this an excorcism."

"Of what? Your good sense? Your morals? Your good name?"

"I'm trying to let go of a man I knew."

Her mother's eyes narrowed.

"Winfield."

"No, not him. It was never him."

"Add lying to the things we don't permit in this household."

"I'll be outside," Zoe said, snapping up her purchases. "If you'd like a cooler or a cigarette, come join me."

After the initial titillation of seeing a man in the all-in-all, *Playgirl* was ho-hum. *Cosmo* depressed her because she got the feeling she was so far off track that she could never catch up—and, besides, she wasn't sure catching up was healthy. The sickly sweet wine cooler gave her the hiccups and bloated her up so that she had to undo the top button of her jeans.

After her solitary foray into vice, Zoe lay on the chaise in the backyard staring up at the stars that had popped up as the sun slipped down the other side of the mountain. The apple trees were offering up their final fruits and made the air smell like the PTA bake sale. The hostas—being nibbled by slugs or not—waved their pale droplet flowers in the cool breeze. So many times she had sat in just this chaise, cooled by just such a breeze, seeing nightfall enter in just this way—with the window in Teddy's room open so that she could hear him playing or make sure he worked on his homework.

She didn't want these elements of her life to change. She loved these parts of her life. But she knew that some things were going to change when Teddy came home. He would ask questions and she would have to answer them.

She loved caring for her mother, loved her town and its hardworking citizens, loved her friends, loved her home, her child; even the simple duties of a church secretary filled her with pride and happiness. But something was missing. She didn't want to believe that she would have to endanger any of what she had to gain something she wasn't sure she would want.

"Oh, Jack, this is where I have to ask you," she murmured to the stars. "Let go of me."

But it was a half-hearted request because just the little bit of Jack—spirit, memory, delusion, whatever—was better than the nothingness.

She heard the back door open and her mother's ponderous progress across the lawn.

"You're holding it wrong," Mrs. Kinnear said, sitting on the chaise beside Zoe. "You're going to burn your pinkie that way. It's not a harmonica, Zoe."

"How would you—"

"Here," her mother said. She picked up the pack of cigarettes, patted out two, stuck them both in her mouth and lit them. Pinching one of the cigarettes between her thumb and index finger, she offered it to her daughter. Zoe took the cigarette warily. "You have to inhale. Here. Like this."

Zoe took a deep drag—and promptly doubled up in a coughing fit. It was as if a small propane torch had been lit just behind her tongue. She swallowed the rest of the bottle of wine cooler, stamped out the cigarette with one foot, and looked up to see the last of her mother's finely etched smoke rings floating up into the canopy of tree leaves.

"Mother!"

"I wasn't always a minister's wife," her mother said coolly. "Zoe, you've missed out on a few things because you've had to be a mother and a nursemaid."

"I love you and Teddy and I wouldn't trade a minute of having you and him at home."

"We've kept you from completing yourself," Mrs. Kinnear said, stamping the cigarette beneath her rubber-soled sandals. "You need a man to complete you. You're not a rule-breaker at heart."

"Women don't need men to—"

"I haven't got the entire female population to worry about—I just have you. And so as your mother, I propose that you do something a little more constructive than ogling naked men in magazines and drinking wine mixed with artificial fruit flavoring. You're going to leave yourself vulnerable in ways you can't imagine if you don't take decisive action."

"What do you suggest?"

"Call Rory Packer back home." She hoisted her girth up. She ignored Zoe's sputtering protests. "Have another wine cooler. Have one more cigarette. Read the *Playgirl,* not that reading's what you do with a magazine like that. Get it out of your system—and then call that good man home."

With the imperial grace of an ocean liner, Mrs. Kinnear walked back into the house.

Zoe closed her magazine, gazed at the stars, picked out her favorite late-summer constellations, and marveled at the unchanging nature of the sky. It had been a terribly long day. Registration for the fall's Sunday school classes had been interminable and the rummage sale meeting had lasted far longer than a rummage sale meeting had a right to. Her mother's suggestion about Rory was worthy of a chuckle. Her suggestion about the second wine cooler was well-taken, but it felt like eating ice cream cones. The first one's great. The second one's okay. And just thinking of the third one made her queasy.

It was in this chaise that Winfield found her. He gathered up the butts on the flagstone patio and put them into the cooler bottle he took out of her limp grasp. Then he picked up the two other empty ones and lined up the three bottles on the back porch steps. He leafed through the *Playgirl*, turning the magazine ninety degrees to the right to regard the centerfold.

For the first time in his life, he thought he could understand why women felt uncomfortable about *Playboy*. Another thing—why would any man pose for a picture wearing nothing more than a cowboy hat and boots? If you were going to wear your boots, you'd already have put on your jeans. And a hat on a naked man was just silly.

Shrugging his shoulders, he tried the *Cosmo*. Now he was in familiar territory. The woman on the cover—hot. The woman on the inside cover ad for some new Revlon product—hot. The woman on the facing page posing with a bottle of perfume—hot.

The woman sleeping on the chaise beside him— hot as seven inches from the midday sun. And she didn't have to tart it up or pout like a scolded child to do it. He ripped the perfume insert out of the magazine and sniffed. Just like the strip club in Bangkok that he had once visited. Putting the magazine down he leaned forward. She smelled like lilies of the valley and Ivory soap. Made him feel like twenty again.

He picked up the magazine. "Sex Tips to Drive Him Wild." Hmmm, wonder what women know that men don't?

He was still uncomfortable with the suit he wore. It was black and very well made, quite expensive actually, but the jacket made his shoulders feel constricted. He had to tug at his pants so that they didn't tug back when he sat down on the second, empty chaise. Also, the movement in sitting caused more spiky pieces of hair to fall down inside his shirt and he had an impulse to rip off his suit jacket and white shirt just so that he could shake the hair off himself like a dog. His head felt light and naked. His feet hurt—if men's dress shoes felt like this, he could only imagine how women's shoes felt. And he'd dearly like one of those cigarettes, even if he had grown accustomed to filterless Turkish Sobraines.

But every environment has its discomfort. On Everest, it's exhausting just to lift one's arm and oxygen masks are enough to turn the most well-adjusted climbers into claustrophic wrecks. In Kenya, the mosquitoes are nearly as big as a man's hand and their bites are correspondingly more painful than that of their itsy-bitsy garden-variety cousins from across the Atlantic.

And in a small town in Colorado, a Sunday-best variety suit pinches a man in all the wrong places, and the tie must be the invention of a sadistic strangler. Win wasn't a complainer, so he couldn't complain. He could only endure.

He was distracted from his discomfort by a piece

of literature that was of the highest interest—informative and searing—gosh, so this is how women learned how to do what they did. He didn't even mind that the only illumination was a back porch light twenty feet away and the stars from a million miles more.

He turned to the article on sex tips meant to drive him wild. Looked at Zoe. Thought the gals in the New York editorial office had it all wrong.

Nine

At first weary glance, he looked like an insurance salesman or maybe an FBI agent. On closer reflection, he looked like Jack Skylar, or what Jack Skylar would have looked like if he hadn't died in a mountain-climbing accident. And if he had decided to get a job as a Calvin Klein model or an insurance salesman or an FBI agent.

It was only when she blinked her eyes a third time at the man in the black suit sitting on the chaise beside her that the awful truth hit her.

She sat bolt upright.

"What happened to your hair?"

Win glanced up from his reading.

"Do you wear matching undies?"

She grabbed for the magazine but he yanked it out of reach.

"I never knew I was supposed to be turned on by matching underwear," he marveled. "I've never noticed a woman's undies. And red, too. I don't suppose you've invested in red underwear? That's supposed to really do the trick. I never noticed."

"You can't tell me you've never seen a woman in her underwear," Zoe said, stretching her fingers tantalizingly close to the magazine. "So give that back."

He held the magazine just inches out of her reach.

"Of course I've seen my fair share of women without their clothes on, and I have to say I've developed a certain preference."

"Oh, really?"

"I like a woman with nothing, absolutely nothing, between me and her flesh."

He stood up, opening the magazine again to what he considered the most interesting page, and announced that although men liked women to talk dirty, that wasn't important to him. In fact, he found it a little embarrassing when a woman turned into a potty mouth.

"And garter belts don't do a thing for me," he said. "Although there was a day, when I was younger, when I felt differently."

"Would you just tell me what you did with your hair?"

"I think you and I could be more compatible now than we ever would have been in our relative youth."

"What did you do with your hair?"

"I got it cut."

"I can see that. But why?"

"And I got a suit," he said. "Don't you like it?"

He turned around once to show her the clean, European-tailored lines.

"I've never owned a suit before," he said. "Wore one of Jack's when I had to."

Well, she did have to admit he looked good in a suit. Heck, he looked like he was made to wear a suit, because he made the suit look good. Just one snag—he was Winfield Skylar. Not a suit sort of guy.

"And another thing, Zoe, I hope you don't wear pantyhose."

"When it's this hot, I don't," she confessed.

"Because I like a bare leg rubbing up against mine under the dinner table."

By some calculation that women often make with men, she ignored what came out of his mouth. Because that wasn't the important thing.

"Where'd you get your suit?"

"In Vail. That's where I got my haircut. A gal named Misty who works at the Salon de Millennium. I sat in a chair next to one of those Trump brothers' girlfriends. Donald, Robert, can't remember which one. Or, at least, this girl—she was getting blond highlights—was a Trump girlfriend during the time I was getting my haircut. I get the feeling that being the girlfriend of a multimillionaire tycoon is a fluid situation. I just hope the relationship lasts long enough so he'll get the chance to see how much blonder she is. Because his girlfriend gave me her home phone number."

"I'm thrilled for you," Zoe said, crossing her arms over her chest in a gesture only slightly less haughty than what she would find herself doing if one of the kindergarteners misbehaved in Sunday school.

"I only found the number when I left the salon. I guess that's what the breast pocket on a suit jacket is for. So that a woman can give her phone number out without incurring embarrassment. Although I can't remember being close enough to her so she could put it in my pocket. Because those foil tips, well, let's just say that the foil tips women wear when they're getting highlights are a definite turn-off."

"I thought you were leaving town."

"Well, I'm not. I keep trying to leave, but I start to miss you. So, I've decided to stay in Sugar Mountain. I'm going to become a gentleman. I have two other suits and a selection of very nice shirts. I might try my hand at business. Or ranching. Or whatever folks around here do to make a living."

"That's wonderful," Zoe said. Her tone suggested quite the opposite sentiment. "Are you going to put your money back into the Sports Shop?"

"Can't. That money's all gone. I'm a poor man. But I figure I'll claw my way to the top of some business—have to think of a business first."

"Where'd the money go?"

"It flew away." Win shrugged. Firmly closing the subject of the Sports Shop, he mused, "Maybe I'll start a photography business. Portraits, weddings, class pictures, and such."

"It wasn't a very profitable business for Rory."

"I'll change that. And if I don't, we'll learn to live within our means."

"We?"

"The three of us. I guess your mother makes four, doesn't she?"

"Oh, no, oh, no. I know what you're thinking, and the answer is no," Zoe said and stood up only to find herself falling, falling, falling into his arms.

"Whoa, there, Zoe, you gotta know something about altitude and alcohol," he said, steadying her. "It's a matter of blood pressure, electrolytes, and oxygenation. You can't drink coolers without something in your stomach; you can't drink three of them if you've never tried 'em before, and you most certainly shouldn't have your first one at anything higher than ten feet above sea level. That's why I gave up drinking."

"You gave up drinking?"

"This party boys drinks tea or coffee."

"You smoke cigarettes. Don't you think they leave a . . ."

She rubbed her tongue along the roof of her mouth.

"Leave a terrible taste, I know."

"Like a dead squirrel's stuck in my throat."

"I've never had a dead squirrel in my throat, so I wouldn't know," he said, pulling a Tic-Tac box out of his breast pocket. He flipped it open and with one hand extracted a mint. She held out her hand. He ignored it, placing the mint on her tongue. As the cool taste spread through her mouth, his finger lingered on her lower lip. "Why'd you dip your toe in the pool of vice?"

She jerked her head away from him.

"I thought it was going to open my eyes, make me feel different, cut me loose. I was starting to feel too old. I thought I missed something. I haven't had that feeling ever before."

She looked at him darkly.

"You put it there," she accused.

"I didn't put anything in you that wasn't already there."

"Oh, my head hurts."

"Sweetheart, this isn't how you try to change your life."

"I'm not trying to change my life," she said, enunciating as best she could. "I want to go back to who I was before you came home."

"Whoa, steady there."

Zoe was experiencing a feeling she suspected was not much different from being hit on the head with a hammer repeatedly. Painful, painful, painful—but not so painful that she didn't struggle out of his arms. He righted her, then let her go. She swayed. Hard.

She put her arms around his waist.

"Win, we talked about this last night. I'm not marrying you. It's a terrible idea."

He smiled down at her, kissing her forehead.

"I'm willing to wait. Willing to court you."

"You're doing this because of Jack."

"Only a little bit."

She wagged a finger at him.

"Let me tell you something, buster. You tell a single soul that Jack is Teddy's father, I'll . . . I'll . . . I'll . . ."

"You don't need to make any threats, Zoe, because I'm not going to tell anyone. It's your business. Yours and Teddy's. When you're ready to tell him or if you're never ready to tell him, that's fine. But since the whole town thinks I'm the dad, I won't have to say a word."

She shook her head.

"Really, I think it wouldn't be a good idea . . ."

"It's a wonderful idea. Now, if you don't have something to eat, that wine's going to leave you with a terrible headache."

"It already has."

Zoe led him into the kitchen. The effects of the cooler were wearing off, replaced with embarrassment.

"Where's my mom?"

"Oh, she saw me when I came in," Win said. "She's a hard case. I don't think the haircut and the suit impressed her."

"Oh, dear, I'll have to talk to her tomorrow."

"Tell her my intentions are honorable. Dinner?"

"I don't have much," she said. "I had planned on going to the grocery store tomorrow."

She stared.

"Oh," she said.

On the counter were three grocery bags with the familiar Lakeside Foods logo.

"The apartment over the Sports Shop has a hot plate, which is perfectly adequate for heating up a can of Spaghetti-Os, but I had a craving for a hamburger. I haven't had a decent hamburger in ten years."

Zoe reached into the nearest bag and pulled out a package of buns, but Win took it away from her.

"Sit down." He pointed to one of the stools on the other side of the island. "Half the fun for me is going to be cooking this."

She sat down and watched him unload the bags.

"Where have you been living that doesn't have hamburgers?"

"All over." Win shrugged. "Most places in the world, a hamburger would be exotic—and too expensive for the average person. Some places, it is a sin to kill a cow. In Bhutan, locals live on tea with yak butter. Sounds better than it tastes." He caught Zoe's look. "Yeah, I know, sounds pretty bad. And in Kenya, I enjoyed chocolate-covered ants."

He needed her help finding a skillet and then again on adjusting the range temperature. Zoe took over the task of chopping onions and they worked companionably as he told her a few other strange customs from around the globe.

"I thought you were leaving."

"With an attitude like that, young lady, they'll never let you run the Welcome Wagon."

"Sorry. I'll try again. When we said good-bye today, I thought it was really good-bye."

"It was. Until I went up to the mountain. That mountain."

"Oh," she said.

"I tried to talk to him."

She sat up straight. Sobered up mighty quick.

"You talked to him?"

"You think you dance with him, don't you? On the mountainside. You think he's near you. You talk about him in the present tense. I thought I'd give it a try, too."

"Did you think he was there?"

"No. I didn't see any ghostly apparitions, no strange noises, no eerie music."

"You don't believe me."

"I believe you. I really do believe you think you talk to Jack."

"I don't talk to him. Well, I talk to him, but he doesn't talk back."

"The only thing I thought I heard . . . oh, nothing. Anyhow, I've decided to move back home to Sugar Mountain."

"Kind of spur-of-the-moment, wouldn't you say?"

"All the best decisions are."

"But you hate this place."

"The alternative is to have us three strike out on our own. World travel is very mind-expanding for a boy Teddy's age."

"We're not doing that. The frying pan's in that cabinet. No, that one. Paige and Kate would miss Teddy and he'd miss them. And all his friends are here and he's happy and it's a great place to raise a child. And then there's my mother. I couldn't have strangers taking care of her."

The phone rang and startled Zoe. Nine o'clock. She lived for nine o'clock, usually counted the minutes, the seconds, from eight-thirty until she heard Teddy's voice. She felt like a traitor as she picked up the phone. She had forgotten.

"Lemonade," she said.

"Lemonade," Teddy said.

"How was camp today?" She asked, glancing at Win's back as he placed the hamburgers on the skillet.

Teddy told her about a water park the camp had visited. It was wet and hot. Zoe wondered aloud about sunscreen. Teddy told her his roommate was a jerk.

"Hey, have you got Kate or Paige over there?" he asked.

"It's not your moms. It's a friend. Winfield. He's making a late dinner."

"Skylar? I thought he was missing."

"He came back."

"And what's he doing at our house?"

"He's a friend of mine. You have your friends over here all the time."

"But that's different."

"Why?"

"Because you're my mom."

There was a long pause.

"Teddy."

"I gotta go, Mom. My roommate wants the phone."

"Teddy, lemonade."

The line was already dead.

Zoe put her fingertips to her temples.

"I blew that one," she said.

Win put a hamburger bun on each of three plates. He topped each with a burger, a piece of lettuce, and a slice of tomato before putting the top of the bun on them.

But there was no *voilà*.

"This is for your mother," Win said. "You can take it upstairs. She said she'd be in her bed. Zoe, are you all right?"

"Just a little worried. I think he feels displaced with TJ and Matt in the picture. He's never had to share any of the three of us. But things aren't the same. And if he thought he had to share me, too, well . . ."

"He'll be home in two days, right?"

Zoe nodded.

"You'll talk to him then. It's just two days."

"It feels like forever."

"That's the mom in you talking. Here, take this plate upstairs to my future mother-in-law."

Zoe didn't even bother to correct him. When she took the plate to her mother's room, she found her mother reading a gardening magazine.

"Is that man still here?" she asked, peering at the plate.

"Winfield. Yes, he's downstairs."

"Heavens! I hope you come to your senses. And soon. I heard the phone ring. How's Teddy?"

"I think he didn't use sunscreen today. They went to a water park."

"Zoe."

"Yes, Mom?"

"I love my grandson so much. I know that grand-mothers, well—you get two of them, and in this case, six, so I'm not really all that important to him."

THE PUBLISHERS OF ZEBRA BOUQUET

are making this special offer to lovers of contemporary romances to introduce this exciting new line of novels. Zebra Bouquet Romances have been praised by critics and authors alike as being of the highest quality and best written romantic fiction available today.

EACH FULL-LENGTH NOVEL

has been written by authors you know and love as well as by up-and-coming writers that you'll only find with Zebra Bouquet. We'll bring y the newest novels by world famous authors like Vanessa Grant, Judy Gi Ann Josephson and award winning Suzanne Barrett and Leigh Greenwood—to name just a few. Zebra Bouquet's editors have selected only the very best and highest quality romances for up-and-coming publications under the Bouquet banner.

YOU'LL BE TREATED

to tales of star-crossed lovers in glamourous settings that are sure to captivate you. These stories will keep you enthralled to the very happy end.

4 FREE NOVELS
As a way to introduce you to these terrific romances, the publishers of Bouquet are offering Zebra Romance readers Four Free Bouquet novels. They are yours for the asking with no obligation to buy a single book. Read them at your leisure. We are sure that after you've read these introductory books you'll want more! (If you do not wish to receive any further Bouquet novels, simply write "cancel" on the invoice and return to us within 10 days.)

SAVE 20% WITH HOME DELIVERY
Each month you'll receive four just-published Bouquet romances. We'll ship them to you as soon as they are printed (you may even get them before the bookstores). You'll have 10 days to preview these exciting novels for Free. If you decide to keep them, you'll be billed the special preferred home subscription price of just $3.20 per book; a total of just $12.80 — that's a savings of 20% off the publisher's price. If for any reason you are not satisfied simply return the novels for full credit, no questions asked. You'll never have to purchase a minimum number of books and you may cancel your subscription at any time.

GET STARTED TODAY –
NO RISK AND NO OBLIGATION

To get your introductory gift of 4 Free Bouquet Romances fill out and mail the enclosed Free Book Certificate today. We'll ship your free books as soon as we receive this information. Remember that you are under no obligation. This is a risk-free offer from the publishers of Zebra Bouquet Romances.

Call us TOLL FREE at 1-888-345-BOOK
Visit our website at www.kensingtonbooks.com

FREE BOOK CERTIFICATE

YES! I would like to take you up on your offer. Please send me 4 Free Bouquet Romance Novels as my introductory gift. I understand that unless I tell you otherwise, I will then receive the 4 newest Bouquet novels to preview each month FREE for 10 days. If I decide to keep them I'll pay the preferred home subscriber's price of just $3.20 each (a total of only $12.80) plus $1.50 for shipping and handling. That's a 20% savings off the publisher's price. I understand that I may return any shipment for full credit-no questions asked-and I may cancel this subscription at any time with no obligation. Regardless of what I decide to do, the 4 Free Introductory Novels are mine to keep as Bouquet's gift.

BN080A

Name _____

Address _____

City _____ State _____ Zip _____

Telephone ( ) _____

Signature _____

(If under 18, parent or guardian must sign.)

Orders subject to acceptance by Zebra Home Subscription Service. Terms and Prices subject to change.

Order valid only in the U.S.

If this response card is missing,
call us at 1-888-345-BOOK.

Be sure to visit our website at
www.kensingtonbooks.com

BOUQUET ROMANCES
Zebra Home Subscription Service, Inc.
P.O. Box 5214
Clifton NJ 07015-5214

"Oh, no, Mother—"

"But fathers—well, for the most part, a boy only gets one. And a father is a very important influence in a boy's life. Teddy needs a father."

"But he's not the father."

"Oh, I know that!"

"You do?"

"You weren't even going out with Rory until Teddy was in preschool."

"Mother, stop thinking about Rory Packer."

Zoe closed the door behind her and went downstairs to the kitchen.

"Did I get any brownie points?" He smiled mischievously.

"No, but she *is* going to eat dinner."

"I'll take what I can get. The way I figure it, when the entire town wants you to marry me, you'll cave in."

"That's what Rory thought, too."

"I've got something Rory doesn't have."

"What?"

"Come here, and I'll show you." He grinned mischievously.

"Oh, no, you're not kissing me again."

"You'll change your mind," he said confidently.

He put the plates down on the kitchen table and offered her a seat.

While they ate their dinner, Win told her more about the world he had seen. Mountain climbs, desert treks, ocean dives, dogsled races. And Zoe felt her unease drift away until she forgot that Teddy hadn't ended his conversation with *lemonade*. When it was nearly midnight, an hour which Zoe had seldom stayed up for, she walked Win out to the porch. Fireflies and mosquitoes danced in the moonlight.

"Good night," he said. And he leaned down to touch the soft hollow of her cheek with the whisper-weight pressure of his lips. He strode down the steps and into the darkness without a backward glance. She ran down to the picket gate.

"I'm sorry you saw me like that," she said. "I've never been drunk."

"Take an aspirin and drink a big glass of water before you go to bed. If you don't, you'll have an unpleasant little reminder of this episode. And remember to ask me to show you one day what you're really missing. It isn't something you can get in a bottle or a magazine or a cigarette pack."

He was halfway to the driveway.

"Hey! Aren't you going to kiss me good night?"

"You didn't use the word *missing*, but close enough," he said and took the walk in three quick strides.

"I wasn't asking you anything," Zoe sputtered as he put his arms around her. "I just thought since you made such a big deal about it last—"

He shut her up with a blazing-hot, five-alarm kiss. He didn't let go of her when she put her hand against his chest and shoved. He didn't let go of her when she wiggled her hips against his embrace. And he most certainly didn't let go when she stopped struggling and opened her mouth to his rich, wet tongue. The only thing that stopped him rom kissing her all night long was the sudden, harp rapping on the second-floor bedroom winlow.

He glanced up.

"Good night, Mrs. Kinnear," he called. A hand ranked the curtain shut. "Zoe, darling, that's what 'ou've been missing. All the rest of it is headache naterial."

He walked down the street, pausing only to wave goodbye at the corner.

Zoe stood, steadying herself with the finial of the picket gate, until even the scent of him, pine and nusky lime, was gone.

Ten

The next morning, Zoe awoke earlier than usual and, thinking of the unair-conditioned classrooms in the back of the church, decided on a crisp, navy blue sundress. She kissed the picture of Teddy and resolved that she would not wait for him to ask her about his father; instead, she would tell him immediately upon his return. That didn't worry her. Explaining to him why he couldn't share this news with anyone—now, that would be the hard part.

She brought her mother a breakfast tray at eight o'clock. Her mother was already awake, writing letters on a lap desk, propped up against a half-dozen pillows. She made a face at the whole-grain cereal, but the doctor had been adamant that sausage and eggs were a thing of the past.

"I'm sorry about last night," Zoe said.

"About which part? The part where you drank in the backyard while smoking cigarettes as if you were a rebellious teenybopper? Or was it perhaps the part about ogling pictures of naked men when you yourself asked Fred to order his assistant manager to take down the *Playboy* calendar over his locker because women had to walk right by it on their way to the ladies' room at the gas station? Or the part where you forgot to bring me ketchup for my hamburger—which was delicious, by the way?"

"All three."

"Zoe, sit down."

"Yes, Mother?"

Her mother scrunched her legs over on the bed so Zoe could sandwich herself between the tray and a stack of magazines. Zoe poured a cup of coffee for her.

"Zoe, about last night, I've been thinking that I've been quite a burden as a mother. And our town has been quite a burden, too, relying on you for every job imaginable. And taking on the responsibilities of being a mother—even if you have always claimed to have Paige and Kate as equal partners—well, it's been a lot. Maybe you need a rest."

"No, Mother, I don't."

"You want a different kind of life."

"I'm happy here."

"I've been thinking about a nursing home."

"Oh, not again."

"I know, I know. I don't want to do it, but perhaps there's a time for it. And maybe it's my time."

"Mother, you want to live at home."

"Sure, but I don't want to take away your chance at happiness."

"Mother, I want to be a good daughter to you. I'm so grateful for all you and Dad did for me, beginning with adopting me and working all the way up to accepting Teddy even when you felt it was wrong to bring a child into the world without a father."

"Zoe, how can Teddy repay you?" Her mother sipped her coffee.

"What do you mean?"

"How can Teddy repay your efforts as a mom?"

Zoe opened her mouth. Closed it. Opened it again.

"Well, he can't, of course. The question's ridiculous—sorry, Mother, but it is. I'm his mother. He doesn't have to repay me."

"Exactly so," her mother said, and took another, more deeply gratifying sip of coffee. "By the way, I don't feel like eating the same breakfast the cows get."

Zoe topped off her mother's coffee and picked up the tray.

"Mother?" She paused at the doorway.

"Yes, darling?"

"I love you."

"I love you, too. And if I absolutely had to accept that Skylar boy in your life, I suppose I could."

"I don't think that will be necessary. I told him last night that I wouldn't marry him."

Mother clasped her hands to her chest.

"Excellent! Now what about Rory?"

"Sorry, Mother, but I'm late. No one else has volunteered to run the kindergarten Sunday school class, so I have to do it again this year. I'll pick you up after the eleven o'clock service."

* * *

When Zoe had to give a talk, whether it was chairing a meeting for the PTA or giving a report to the Village Council on the success of the blood drive, she worried and fretted. Wrote down notes that seemed perfectly sensible at the time but which, when faced with a group, were utterly useless. So she admired the reverend because, although he had his shortcomings on managing a church, he always prepared his sermons with great care and delivered them in a manner of a chat between friends. Every week, more than a few people thought the reverend was talking in a special language just to them about the things that concerned them most.

Besides his ability to speak every Sunday morning, Zoe admired him for visiting the children in their Sunday school classrooms before the service. Knowing he only had ten minutes before he had to dash to the pulpit, she gathered the kindergarteners on the rug and put Mac Tucker, the most rambunctious one, on her lap. Reverend Martin sat on a stool that would have been Baby Bear's if Baby Bear had been a church-goer.

"How many of you will be starting school this fall?" the reverend asked, affecting surprise and delight when every kid raised a hand. "It's a very exciting time. You're going to have so much fun in kindergarten! Mrs. Medow is a wonderful teacher. And starting something new, like school or a relationship—" He looked at Zoe "—is also kind of scary. Some kids, even adults, have trouble taking chances. But we are so lucky to have so many people who care for us, who won't mind if we make mistakes, and who will still love us if we fail. Can you name somebody who cares about you?"

Several raised hands.

"My mom," Katie said. "And my dad."

"My grandma," Michael said.

"God," said another kid, one of the Cook children, an advanced one.

"Those are good answers," he said. "Anybody else? Yes, Cindy, do you have someone who cares about you?"

"No," she said. "I mean, yes, but I have a question."

"We're here to answer your questions," the reverend said earnestly.

"Who's that man in the cemetery?"

The reverend twisted around in his chair. Everyone stared out the window, past the jungle gym and the wire fence to the moss-covered stones that told of Sugar Mountain residents past.

"That's one of the Skylar brothers," the reverend said. "His name is Winfield. He used to live here."

"Why isn't he in church?" the Cook boy asked. "Is he digging new graves?"

"He's gardening!" Katie said.

"Yeah, he's got a shovel like my mother's," Mac said, craning his neck to see. "My parents say it's wrong to work on a Sunday. It's the rest day. He's supposed to be in church."

"Well, he's not working," the reverend said. "He's worshipping. He's just doing it in a different way."

Zoe slid Mac Tucker off her lap. She went to stand in the doorway leading to the playground. The reverend told a parable, a story in the Bible which would, no doubt, include a kid going into kindergarten. She wanted to walk across the playground to the cemetery but knew she couldn't leave her classroom.

The stones marking Jack's grave and that of the long-dead Skylar patriarch had never been neglected. A person bringing a bouquet of flowers for a much-missed loved one was just as likely to bring an extra one for the Skylars. But the cemetery as a whole was unforgivingly austere, its only maintenance being a bi-monthly mowing of the lawn by either Zoe or any teenager wanting to make a fast ten bucks out of the Holy Comforter petty cash drawer.

Win was planting hostas, black-eyed Susans, and rodgersia—three woodland perennials that spread their foliage and deepen their roots each season.

He looked up once, seeming to notice that he was being watched. He waved in greeting, but did not stop his labors. The reverend wound up his story and asked the kids to check if he had food between his teeth. He asked the same question every week, and without fail, it made the kids giggle to think of him worrying about people paying attention to his teeth and not his sermons. When he left, Zoe took his place in the chair with its back to the window.

Before she picked up her mother that morning, she went back to the cemetery, but Win was not there. His newly formed garden was like a prayer, beautiful and serene.

That afternoon, Zoe paid a visit to the Skylar home. She knocked on the door. Rang the doorbell. Pulled on the dinner bell on the back porch.

"Mrs. Skylar, I know you're in there!"

But there was no answer.

Zoe left a cardboard box on the front steps. In it was everything a grandmother would need to be introduced to Teddy.

There was hardship in many of the endeavors that Win had undertaken in his career. Broken arm, two bouts with malaria, hunger, fatigue . . . and then there were excruciating experiences of a different sort.

Win waited outside the post office trailer at seven o'clock on Monday morning, and after evading a punch in the jaw, he persuaded Kurt that his intentions were honorable. Kurt rubbed the gravel off his chest and took the hand Win offered. When both men were upright, Kurt reluctantly shook hands.

Nonetheless, he declined to unlock the postal trailer.

"Honorable?"

"Absolutely."

Kurt reared back, shoved his regulation summer pith helmet back off his forehead, and gave Win the once-over. Twice.

"What'd you do to your hair?"

"It's not any shorter than yours."

"But I'm a federal employee. You are a ne'er-do-well."

Win sighed.

"And that suit's pretty snappy."

"I think it makes me look respectable."

"Makes you look like a gigolo."

"How do you know what a gigolo looks like?"

"I saw the movie."

"What movie?"

After an extensive conversation about Hollywood and its cinematic offerings of the past several decades, it was established that Kurt simply thought Win looked a little too dressed up for Sugar Mountain.

Kurt glanced up at the sun.

"On a day that promises to hit ninety in the shade, I think you're going to sweat. By the way, what are you doing here?"

"I want to marry Zoe."

"Are you the father?"

"Well, if I said I wasn't, you'd try to punch me again, wouldn't you?" Win asked.

"I suppose," Kurt conceded, rubbing the pain off his knuckles. "So, what do you want with me?"

"I know how mail works."

"Yeah?"

"It's magical."

Kurt had thought pretty much the same thing all the twenty years he had been in the service of the post office. He grunted noncommittally.

"A postman knows his route," Win said.

"Postal carrier," Kurt corrected, although his heart wasn't with the strictly correct nomenclature. There was something about the word *postman* that stirred his soul; and when Win used the word, Kurt thought he might, just might, have been mistaken in his opinion of the Skylar brother.

"A postman knows everyone in town," Win said. "And he's held in universal high regard. Everyone looks forward to the daily visit of the postman. He's a stabilizing influence on the community. For some older people, the postman might be the only person they speak to for several days. A simple nice-weather-we're-having or those-flowers-are-blooming-pretty from a postman can be essential to health and happiness. The postman is the first to know if someone's having trouble. He's like a shepherd watching over a flock."

"Hmmmm. That's true, and it annoys me so much when people use that phrase *goin' postal*. It seems a sacrilege. But your point is?"

"I'd like a favor."

Kurt's eyes narrowed.

"I don't think so."

"This is a favor only a bona fide postal official can do for me."

"If it involves the delivery of mail that has not been properly stamped, it's a no go."

"Nothing like that," Win said smoothly. He touched the toe of his dress shoes very gently against the smoky grey duffel bag beside Kurt's car. "Now, that's a mighty big bag of mail you have to sort through. Do you get this big a delivery every day?"

"Dropped off from central sorting every morning at 4:00 A.M."

"Well, why we don't we take it inside where we can talk?"

"I know Alex is only seven years old," Kathy Clark said. "But I want him in the fourth grade Sunday school."

"We talked about this last week. He's in second grade," Zoe pointed out for the fifth time during the conversation.

"He's advanced."

"He's not that advanced," Zoe said and then, seeing Kathy's wounded look, amended, "Of course, I've heard he's really smart. That the teachers give him extra math problems."

"He was reading when he was two."

"I've heard."

"I didn't even help him. He just picked up a book and started reading."

Actually, Zoe had heard the usual gossip that Kathy Clark had spent hours every day with a set of flash cards and a bag of jelly beans. Alex Clark, sitting now on the couch with one of the Harry Potter books, was undeniably smart—and undeniably overindulged in candies of all sorts.

"And he's not just intellectual." Kathy leaned forward, dropping her voice to a whisper. She smelled strongly of Jean Naté. "He's spiritually advanced."

"There are a lot of very bright kids in Sugar Mountain."

"He's brighter than any of 'em."

"Kathy, I'm not registering him for fourth grade and that's that," Zoe said. "He'll be happier with kids his own age."

Alex looked up from his book.

"I'm talking to the reverend about this," Kathy said.

Zoe leaned forward so that she could see a sliver of the inside of the office across the hall.

"He's in, so go right ahead," Zoe said. "I'll just leave the grade blank until you finish talking."

"Come along, Alex," Kathy said sharply and the two Clarks left Zoe's office. Alex looked back once and shrugged in a way that Zoe knew was meant as an apology for the trouble his mother caused.

Five minutes later, the reverend poked his head into Zoe's door. Before he could say a word, the front door of the rectory slammed loudly.

"Second grade?" Zoe asked.

The reverend nodded.

"Didn't we have this conversation with her last week?"

"Yes. And last year, too. Every year she does this. Poor Alex must get really tired of being so advanced."

"Don't you get tired of listening to her?"

"No, because I like her."

"She's tough to like."

"She's a softy. Tomorrow, she'll just happen to have an extra dozen cookies hot out of the oven, which she will just happen to want to share with us."

"Oh, yeah, she does make good . . ." The reverend stared at something just beyond Zoe's shoulder. "Well, would you look at that!"

Zoe turned around to look through the window. Across the street, Kurt the mailman stood talking to Mrs. Greenough. Zoe glanced at her watch—eleven thirty-five, and Kurt was right on schedule.

"Kurt must have half the block out there talking with him," the reverend said. "You know, he's like that. Always talking—it's a wonder he gets the mail delivered by noon."

But it was not Kurt who caused her to rise from her desk chair with a start. It was not Kurt who caused her to press her fist against her mouth to halt an untoward word. It was not Kurt who caused her to bolt past the reverend with unseemly determination.

"And who is that guy carrying Kurt's mail pouch?" the reverend asked, following her. "I've sure never seen him in church . . . Zoe, Zoe, where are you going, Zoe?"

Zoe yanked the front door open so hard the stained glass rattled. She ran across the street, barely pausing as William Woo, the carpenter, shoved his foot down—hard—on the brakes of his truck in order to avoid hitting her.

The cause of all her troubles was standing on the street corner.

"Darling, you're looking lovely today," Win said. "But I really think you should take your hair out of that bun because it's such a beautiful color. Don't you agree, Mrs. Greenough?"

"What are you doing?"

"He's helping me carry the mail," Kurt said. "Do you know how heavy that darned bag is?"

On Win's shoulder was slung a mail pouch bulging with envelopes. He wore a white shirt and a loosened silk tie, but had ditched the suit jacket he had worn Saturday evening. Although droplets of sweat were noticeable on Kurt's upper lip and forehead, Win looked relaxed and cool, totally at ease—everything, in fact, that Zoe was not.

"What are you doing?" she repeated.

"I'm having a chat."

There was Mrs. Greenough; Mrs. Greenough's next-door neighbor; Mrs. Johnson, who lived two doors down; the lady who lived across the street; Mrs. Smith, who lived . . . well, it was like a block party. Except it was on a Monday morning, and there wasn't any potato salad. And when two ladies walked up from the corner it became a two-and-a-half-block party.

"I'm so happy for you," Mrs. Johnson said and put her beefy arms around Zoe. She squished Zoe's face against her breast. "Congratulations!"

Oh, darn, thought Zoe.

"It's not congratulations to the bride," Mrs. Greenough said peevishly. "You're supposed to congratulate the groom and give best wishes to the bride."

Oh, double darn, thought Zoe.

"Otherwise, it makes it sound like the bride caught him," Mrs. Smith said.

Oh, double double darn, thought Zoe.

She pulled out of Mrs. Johnson's embrace only to be thrust into the Eau d'Amour aura of Mrs. Smith.

"Best wishes," Mrs. Smith whispered. "A gal needs best wishes because the state of holy matrimony is a holy terror!"

The neighborly ladies giggled.

"I sure hope it isn't going to be like your last engagement," Mrs. Johnson confided.

Zoe looked over the floral print shoulder of Mrs. Smith. Win looked rather pleased with himself.

"How many people have you talked to this morning?"

"I've been delivering mail with Kurt since eight o'clock," Win boasted. "Your mother wasn't there, but we noticed she's won a Mediterranean cruise for two."

"She's a semifinalist," Zoe said. "She's always a semifinalist. That's how those things work."

"We only have four more houses to go and we'll be done with all of Sugar Mountain."

He reached into the pouch and pulled out a dozen envelopes held together with a rubber band.

"This is for the church," he said.

"Damn you, Winfield!"

Mrs. Smith relinquished her.

Mrs. Greenough touched her hand to her chest as if to stave off pain.

"Oh, dear," Mrs. Johnson's said, her eyes widening to dessert plate size.

Mrs. Smith crossed herself elaborately, though Mrs. Smith was raised Methodist and had only seen people crossing themselves when the Pope's recent visit to America was aired on cable.

And Kurt the mailman shook his head and said soulfully, "His habits are rubbing off on her."

"Why, Zoe, darling, I don't believe I've ever heard you swear," Win said calmly.

Eleven

His righteousness was positively enough to make her swear a second time.

"Damn you."

"Never took you to be such a potty mouth. But after seeing how you can belt down a drink, smoke a cigarette, and look at pictures of naked men, I just shouldn't be surprised."

"You pulled a Rory Packer."

"I didn't mean to. Just like I'm sure you didn't mean to swear."

"But you did pull a Rory."

"It didn't start off that way."

"But it ended up that way."

"Yes," Win said, sighing aggrievedly. "I guess it is a Rory Packer."

"You know what I'm going to have to do."

"Well, there's a problem. You can't call the Sugar Mountain *Chronicle* and have them print a retraction for an engagement announcement that they never printed."

"No, but I can . . . oh, no."

"You figured it out. You'll have to speak to every postal customer in Sugar Mountain."

"I should make you do it."

He rubbed his shoulder.

"I think I've pulled a muscle," he said.

"You did not."

"Maybe so. But you can't send me out there to-morrow. You have to be the one. Otherwise, who knows what I'll announce next."

She repeated her swear word of choice.

Win chuckled.

"You can carry Kurt's bag for four hours," he continued, rubbing his shoulder. "Heavy for a woman as diminutive as you, but maybe he'll be a gentleman and share the load. Then again, maybe he won't."

"You don't like him."

"He's tough to take after the first thirty seconds or so. It was excruciating. He holds the envelopes up to the sunlight and he has better X-ray vision than Superman. He shakes boxes to see if he can figure out what's inside a package. Furthermore, that man knows more about the history of the post office than it's healthy to. And he wants to share it all with me."

"That's why I can't marry you."

"Because the guy's an encyclopedia of postal Post-its?"

They sat in her office, after she had with unchar-acteristic brusqueness told the reverend to sort the mail himself. She had shut the door, and the door to her office had not been closed—ever. She had,

over the course of the last minute, heard the mur-
mur of women in the hallway asking the reverend
if it were too late to register their children for Sunday school and he had murmured something which
had sounded like "come back later" or "she's in
there with that Winfield boy, you heard they're getting married, right?"

Zoe positively vibrated with anger on the couch,
a donation from the Burlesons' basement rumpus
room, and Win sat across from her on the coffee
table. She didn't have the spare indignation to tell
him that he was sitting on her notes for the Winter
Pageant meeting this afternoon, but maybe it was
just that she thought she'd start screaming at him
if she said anything at all about it.

"Marriage is a serious thing," she said carefully.

"I know."

"It should not be undertaken lightly."

"This sounds like the opening words to our nuptials."

She raised her hand to silence him in the same
manner she often used to quiet a roomful of kindergarteners on a Sunday morning. It was really a
very effective gesture.

"You cannot marry me simply because I had your
brother's child."

"There's also loving you."

"And I told you before that loving me means loving Sugar Mountain. Even you can't say you love
Libby Joyce."

"No, I can't say I love her, but you're too selfless.
A marriage is just two people; it's not a municipal-

ity. Can't I love just you? Just you. I do, you know. Love you."

Her heart stopped a beat, but then she got hold of herself.

Love her?

"You're just saying that."

He raised his head.

"I'm hopelessly in love," he said wearily. "You have followed me everywhere. The most remote parts of the world, the highest mountains, the hottest deserts, the wettest jungles."

"I've stayed right here."

"You're how I decide on the color of my car—always red—or the books I read—always something I think you'd like. You're how I make up my mind to help someone. I've always had you as a memory in my heart. But now, I've seen you again. And I thought I was asking you to marry me for selfless reasons. But really, I wanted that bond between us to be real and not just in my mind. Because I love you. And now, damn it, I'm trapped. I can't leave you. And you don't want me to stay."

"You can go anytime you want."

"No, I can't. Because I'd miss you. And this time it wouldn't be an intellectual thing. It wouldn't be a way of motivating myself to work harder or go further. It would be a feeling that would give me no rest."

He looked almost angry about the notion. She wasn't any more delighted than he at the prospect. They both considered the oath she had uttered, the

ne that had caused the street to clear in thirty
:conds flat.

"Win, you can't possibly love me, because you
on't know who I am now," she said, and her deli-
ate, unpolished hands fluttered in an encompass-
1g gesture that at first made Win consider the
ffice, cheerful but worn. Then the church, homely
ut welcoming. And then the street beyond the win-
ow. Four boys, baseball caps worn backwards, sped
y on their bikes. Cicadas chirped. A pickup truck
aded with feed bags drove by.

"I'm a mother. I'm a daughter. I'm a secretary.
m a PTA volunteer. I'm the kind of woman who
oes a good job with things. I'm a small-town
oman who fits right into a small town. And I hap-
en to have had a relationship with your brother.
. short but very intense relationship. And I turned
p pregnant."

"I don't care what kind of job you have. I think
's great you volunteer—somebody has to do it or
le town collapses. I can understand your falling
or Jack because every girl who got within a hun-
red yards of him did, too. All I was trying to do
nis morning was to meet everyone in your miser-
ble, sorry-ass town," he said, standing up. He
aced. "I talked to everyone. Politely. I told them
bout wanting to do the right thing. I didn't even
ave to mention the word marriage. They knew
hat I meant—and sure, most people said it wasn't
good idea."

"Why not?"

"Because they think like I do—that you're too

good for me. I think Mr. Barron still didn't believe me when I told him I didn't throw mud balls at his windows fifteen years ago."

"Oh, that again. That man never forgets."

"And once the word *marriage* came up, it was tough to get everyone to stop talking. The lady at the bakery even said she'd bake the cake for our reception."

"Cake happy, that's what she is. She'd bake a cake if you told her you were celebrating the fact that it was Tuesday."

"I could learn to like these people. I really could."

"Win, there's another reason we can't marry."

"Let me guess—it's because you don't love me," he said.

She hesitated.

What was love? Respect and admiration, shared interests, agreed-upon values, mutual courtesies—these words would have formed her definition if someone writing a dictionary had asked her opinion last Monday. But in a week's time, there had been a kiss. And another. And another. Seriously discombobulating kisses. Her face grew hot as she considered those kisses. And all they could have led to.

"Zoe," he said, brightening.

"I didn't say a word."

"No, it's all over your face. Darling, you love me. That's the best news I've heard in years. Let's go get that reverend."

"No, no, no, I don't want to . . . Win, I don't love you."

"No?"

"No," she said firmly. "It'd be better if you went wherever it is in the world that you're going. Now would be a good time to leave."

"Kiss me, Zoe."

She recoiled.

"What?"

He knelt in front of her.

"I said *kiss me.*"

She laughed uneasily.

"Why should I?"

"Because your kisses betray your feelings."

"Kissing has nothing to do with it. Love is about respect and shared interests and . . ."

He puckered his lips as if he had bit into a lemon.

"Kiss me. Then start that respect and shared interests thing again. And I'll go. Leave you alone. I'll nurse my lonely love but I'll at least know that it was never meant to be. But only if you kiss me first."

"I won't do it," she said, crossing her arms over her chest.

"Isn't this worth taking the risk of one, just one, more kiss?"

The request was one that, if written in a pleading note, would have been flatly rejected. The idea was preposterous. The notion of kissing a man just to determine whether there was a possibility of the development of lifelong love and devotion? Kissing him to decide if he should be the father of her ten-year-old son? Kissing him to see whether she was in love?

No way!

But Win had, from his birth, the most extraordinary smile. Not a grin, not a sneer, not a mile wide nor so tight as to be insincere. It was a distinctly masculine smile, knowing and sexy and boyish and just the slightest bit asymmetrical.

That smile had never been refused.

"You are too charming," she said uneasily.

"I hope so."

"But, Win, you have to promise me that this nonsense about marriage will stop right after I tell you that I don't love you."

He hushed her with the feather-light touch of his mouth. Her lips pressed together firmly, dry and unrelenting. He leaned back. Regarded her carefully.

"You have to close your eyes for this to work."

"Oh, sorry."

Her lashes fluttered and dropped, shading her flushed cheeks. He took a deep breath, tensing as he thought of how much was at stake. He had to persuade her, had to marry her, had to give her son a father, and then—here is where he thought about what he needed most—he had to have a home to come to, for he had spent so much of himself out in the wide world. It was the first time he had ever thought of the word *home* without derision—he startled himself.

He laid one hand on the back of the couch, the

fingertips of his other hand coming to rest lightly on her shoulder. He wondered if she felt Jack's presence now, and if she did, would he, too, feel Jack as a third presence in this quiet office.

This introspection was intense, yes, but brief. Very brief. For he was a man of action, often making quick decisions between courses of danger and survival. And he made one now.

He kissed her. At first, his lips were tight and he was infused with an unaccountable nervousness. Then some instinct—of giving up all thought— kicked in. In ten years in as many countries, he had tasted many women's lips. He wasn't promiscuous; he wasn't a predator; it simply happened that way. She had accused him of being charming, and he was. And so, he was used to kisses that were generously, even aggressively, given to him.

This was not her way. She seemed to struggle within herself before tentatively opening her lips, and when she did, he felt a softness and sweetness in her surrender. He tasted all her mouth; and when he felt her tongue dart between his lips, he was surprised and thrilled. Her arms had found their way around his neck; her legs were almost on top of his, and if he just put his arms around her waist, he could pull her up on top of him.

He had her.

He had his bride.

He had kissed her senseless and he'd walk her across the hall to the reverend and get the deed done before she had time to think . . .

Abruptly, he was holding . . . nothing. She was

standing at the window with her back to him, furiously shoving bobby pins into a halo of curls that had fallen around her shoulders.

"This was a good idea," she said. "It's at last proved to you that marriage is impossible. I appreciate the offer; I truly do. But I do not love you, as you can very well see from our kiss."

He opened his mouth, but no words came out.

"You should just go back wherever you . . . well, I don't want you to feel unwelcome. You're welcome to stay in Sugar Mountain, but of course, not as my husband. Or my boyfriend. Or Teddy's father. Or any of the things that kiss might make you think of. Let's just be friends, okay?"

"Just be friends?" Win muttered. He was a man, and all over the world, in every language and every nation, a woman saying "just be friends" to a man meant "I don't love you, not one little bit." It was the worst thing to hear, followed only by "I really value your friendship" and "I'll always think of you fondly."

"I really value your friendship," Zoe said. "And I'll always think of you fondly."

"But I thought . . . I thought," he sputtered. "It's just I thought . . . I thought that was a damn fine kiss. You can't tell me you didn't feel anything. And the other times I've kissed you . . ."

"Kisses are not all there are to a relationship."

"Then we should make love."

If he expected her to turn around and stride over to give him a well-deserved slap on the face, he was disappointed. She merely shrugged, back to him, and said mildly, "You are purposely misunderstanding my meaning. If you want to talk about respect, mutual admiration, shared interest—"

"Don't bother," he said miserably.

There was a knock on the door, tentative at first, and then again, bolder.

"Yes?" Zoe said, stabbing the last of her bobby pins in place and smoothing the front of her navy blue dress.

The reverend poked his head inside.

"Hate to interrupt you two lovebirds."

"We're not lovebirds," Zoe said. "We're friends."

"Best of friends," Win said. He put his face in his hands.

The reverend took off his glasses, fogged them with a *ha!* on each lens, and rubbed them clean on the sleeve of his light cardigan.

"It's okay. You don't have to hide your relationship with Win any longer."

"Reverend, there's nothing to hide."

"Won't do you any good to deny it," Win moaned. "Didn't do any good eleven years ago, and it won't do any good now. Trouble is, everyone else thinks you love me."

"Denial is not always the right path," the reverend continued. "But that's not why I'm here. We've got six women out here who are using up their lunch hour waiting to register their children. You know, Mr. Eckhardt is a fine man but he's awfully persnickety about his clerks punching the time clock."

"I'll get right on it," Zoe said crisply.

Win rubbed his lips.

"Does this mean no?" he asked.

"That's right. No."

"Forever no?"

"Forever no."

"You didn't feel a damn thing—sorry, reverend—darn thing when I kissed you?"

"Not a thing."

She stepped past him to welcome the women into her office. In that moment, her scent—lily of the valley and Ivory soap—caused him to raise his head out of his hands.

When he did so, he noticed something that caused him to put away despair.

Just friends, eh? he thought.

Best of friends, huh?

Think of me fondly?

That blush, Miss Zoe, is the color of a certain Chevrolet Impala that I owned in my youth, he thought. *And it tells me everything, everything I need to know.* He swallowed back the urge to celebrate.

"I'll be going now," he said woodenly.

"Overseas?" the reverend inquired.

"Oh, no, I'm just leaving her office. I'm actually thinking of making my home in Sugar Mountain."

"Really?" the reverend said. "How marvelous."

Zoe paused in the doorway, her back to the two men. Her spine stiffened. She did not turn around to look at them.

"I'm thinking of opening a photography business," Win said. "I've played around with the camera a little."

"There's a need for it. Folks like to have a pretty wedding picture to put on their desks."

"You don't have any openings in your Sunday choir, do you?"

"We have had a certain lack in tenors."

"And Sunday school? I mean, I want to fully integrate myself into the community," Win said.

"You'd have to take some classes. I'd suspect that church dogma isn't your strong suit."

"True. That might be a problem," Win allowed. "Maybe I should be an usher instead . . . wonder what I said to make Zoe so upset."

The two men stared at the door and, with the most masculine of instincts, braced themselves for the sound of a hard, glass-shattering slam.

Twelve

"Women," Win said.

"Oh, they're not so bad," TJ said.

"I didn't say they were bad. Just mysterious. Strange. Like they're . . . like they're . . . like they're from another planet."

"Mars," Mayor Stern said confidentially. Assuming an invitation, he sat down at the table and took a taste of his own onion loaf. Nodding at its perfection, he swallowed quickly and explained to the three Skylar brothers, "Women are from Mars. I read it in a book."

"Women are not from Mars," Sheriff Matt corrected. "Men are from Mars. Venus is the woman planet."

"I didn't know the planets had sexes," TJ said, smacking his lips at the tart lemonade they shared.

"They don't," Matt said. "It's that women and men have different ways of communicating. The different planets is a metaphor for the human condition."

"I didn't know you believed in extraterrestrials, either," TJ said.

Matt jogged his sheriff's cap.

"I don't! It's that there's this book that says . . . oh, I give up."

"Whatever." The mayor shrugged. "You guys want another pitcher of lemonade?"

"No, I have to go," TJ said. "My Venusian has her first sonogram scheduled for this afternoon. I'm hoping for a Martian; but if it's healthy and has all its antennae intact, I don't care."

"How 'bout you, Sheriff?"

Matt shook his head.

"Kate's taking me to the ballet in Denver. Two-hour drive when I'd rather stay home and watch the Broncos, but it's supposed to be a good ballet."

"No such thing as good ballet," the mayor pointed out.

"Kate really likes that stuff."

"Women," Win repeated.

"Win, I'm glad you're going to do the right thing," TJ said. "Teddy is your son. He needs a father, and Zoe doesn't deserve to pine away for you all her life."

"She hasn't been pining," Matt said.

"Hard to tell with that gal, she's so strong and steady," the mayor opined.

"She'll be a stabilizing influence on your life," Matt added. "She's an easy woman to love. So wonderful, so sweet. You know, they say a good man's hard to find, but a good woman's just as rare."

"What if I told you—" Win said.

"I'm thinking of getting married myself," Mayor Stern interrupted abruptly.

The three Skylar brothers stared, mouths open.

"You know Sharmaine, right?"

The three Skylar brothers nodded. It was very difficult to keep up with the mayor's girlfriends. There were so many of them, the mayor could set up a revolving door on his front porch. Not one Skylar brother knew who Sharmaine was. But none of them was willing to interrupt the narrative to ask.

"Anyhow, you know she's a stewardess, right?" The three men nodded in unison. "So, whenever she does the Denver-Toronto route, she brings back two bottles of duty-free champagne. We drink one bottle to celebrate."

"Celebrate what?" Matt asked. He grunted. "Ouch! TJ, why'd you kick me?"

"Tuesday, Wednesday, or whatever day of the week she flies in, that's something to celebrate," the mayor said.

"What do you do with the other bottle?" TJ asked.

"She puts it under my bed." The mayor leaned back, sighing. "She says when the floor under my bed is filled up with bottles, we'll have enough to hold the reception."

"Oh," TJ said. "Didn't understand the bottle thing. Thought for a minute it was a religious custom."

"So, how are you going to break up with her when the floor under the bed is full of champagne bottles?" Matt asked. Matt had worked as sheriff under the mayor's reign for so long that he thought he knew his boss well.

"I'm going to marry her."

The men were silent for a long, solemn moment. The news was shocking. It would crush the hopes of a dozen Sugar Mountain women who pined for the dashingly handsome elected official.

"She's the first woman who ever asked me without a frying pan held over my head," the mayor said. "We're just about there, guys. I might have to take that long, lonely walk down the aisle."

"It's the bride who does that part," Matt said.

"Zoe's gonna marry me," Win said abruptly. "It's just taking a little longer to close the deal."

"She's just cautious, that's all," TJ said.

"She's trying to make sure you're not doing it when you don't want to. But you want to," Matt said pointedly. "You'd better want to."

"Guys, what if it were Jack in my place?"

The mayor's eyebrows knitted together.

"You mean, running out on a woman who was carrying his child?" Matt asked, horrified. "He wasn't like that."

"And why do you think I am?"

"The difference is Jack would never make love to a woman without taking precautions," Matt said. "And he never took advantage of anyone. Especially someone as young and sheltered as Zoe."

"He was honorable," the mayor agreed.

"Why do you think I'm not honorable?" Win demanded.

"Because you were always a troublemaker," TJ said, with just a hint of sibling pomposity. "Dropping out of high school, tooling around in that bright red convertible, staying out till all hours, worrying Mother sick . . ."

"And what about throwing mud balls at Tom Barron's house?" Mayor Stern asked.

"I never—"

"I'd lay odds you were drinking alcohol before you were twenty-one," Matt said. "I'm just thankful that there's never been any drug trafficking in Sugar Mountain, because you would have been just the sort of kid to experiment."

Win stood up.

"I'm outta here," he said. "Have a great time at the ballet. And send my best wishes to Paige for a good sonogram."

"When's your wedding?" Mayor Stern asked. "Because if Matt and I have to close off the streets in front of the church, we gotta have some notice. Win, don't run off like that. You have to try my onion loaf. Jeez Louise, he looks awfully pissed-off for a guy planning his wedding."

The car had air-conditioning—a blessing as it was over a hundred on the hell index. After fighting with the lock on the driver-side door for a minute, he slumped in the car. The good part was next—turning the cool air up until condensation droplets developed on the vents.

As the temperature in the car dropped, so did his anger.

"Women are from Mars." He chuckled. "That's a new one"

There were plenty of things about America that he had only read about, in magazines that often reached his part of the world months after their publication. Cabbage Patch dolls. Beanie Babies. Barbra Streisand getting married. Four or five *Star Trek* sequels seemed to be reviewed and all had the same plot, near as he could tell. Then there were a half-dozen scandals in Washington and a couple more in Hollywood. He didn't understand—heck, didn't even know about—the latest skirmishes in the battles of the sexes.

When he got out of the parking lot of Mayor Stern's tavern, black tar oases appeared and disappeared every fifty feet. Smart folks were sitting in the shade of porch eaves and shop window awnings, and near genius types were napping in air-conditioned bedrooms or leafing through back issue magazines in the library, which was kept at a uniform sixty-five degrees.

The streets were empty and that was just as well because he didn't want to have to tip a hat he didn't have on his head or wave a hand at someone just because they had been born in the same longitude and latitude as he had. He didn't doubt he could live in Sugar Mountain, even live here for the rest of his life. He didn't doubt he could be a father to Teddy—and do his brother Jack proud.

But most of all, he didn't doubt, not for one minute, that she would marry him. He'd ask her again to marry him after they made love. That'd be just the right time, he figured, since that's when the few women who had asked him had asked him. He had no doubt that she'd say yes then, because he'd been tempted himself on those few tender occasions.

He'd seen that blush. That bright popping-red blush. She wasn't as immune to him as she'd like to believe. He was faintly respectable looking in his suit, even if the jacket was a folded-up memory in the back seat. He had a day and a half until Teddy came home, and then she wouldn't be the sort to stay out late. 'Course if he were married to her, there wouldn't be any need for staying out late. All he needed was the right atmosphere. Something that he would have called, in his youth, a "love shack." Second floor over the Sports Shop wasn't what he had in mind.

He drove north, past the Little Lilac tearoom, the gas station, the library, the post office (shuttered tightly, with a window unit roaring even though Kurt was long since gone). He passed two blocks of Cape Cod-inspired houses and the painted-lady Victorian of the Cruikshank sisters. Then the spaces between houses grew wider, until he was driving along the ranchers' fields, and within the hour he had accomplished his mission and was driving back to town.

Then, just as he sped past a sign informing him that he was entering Sugar Mountain Village and

here were 250 folks who called it home, that was
when he felt it.

It wasn't much for an otherworldly experience.
Nothing he could have explained. Nothing he
couldn't have explained away.

And yet, there it was. A feeling of weight beside
him, although the plush leather cushion of the passenger seat gave no evidence of a rider—invisible,
otherworldly, heavenly, or extraterrestrial. No, no,
here was nothing more than a sensation of someone, the sort of thing that made Win instinctively
and politely move his right elbow off the armrest
between the seats. And there was the scent of the
Beechnut gum that Jack used to chew.

"I could use a little help here, buddy," Win said
after a few minutes. "Nothing big, just some back-
ing off of Zoe. And by the way, why is it that everyone here is happy to believe I'm a jerk but would
never think the same thing about you? Is it just
because you're dead or is it because you really were
so much better than me?"

He looked around but the car was empty.

"It should have been me that she made love to,"
he said aloud. "I should be Teddy's father. I would
have married her and made a good husband . . ."
He felt a very funny sensation, as if skepticism were
a palpable smell not unlike rotten eggs. "Okay, at
least, I think I would have married her. And I could
have been an okay husband." The sulfurous smell
grew more intense. "All right, I would have made
a good-faith effort."

He leaned over to the glove compartment,

popped it open, and took out a green cardboard cut in the shape of a pine tree. It was an air freshener he had ripped off the rearview mirror when he had first purchased the car. He pressed it to his nose but it did no good.

"All right, Jack, it's true. I would have made a rock-bottom, low-as-mud husband. I needed to travel; I needed to climb; I needed to push myself to every limit. It's a damn good thing that I never kissed her when she was young, buddy, because if I had, it would have been me she loved."

He didn't know if that last part were true, but suddenly the car smelled like the air freshener—but not as sickly sweet nor as cloying—instead, it was like morning on the mountains, when dewdrops clung to the lowest branches of the evergreens.

He threw the air freshener back into the glove compartment.

Ahead of him he saw a blue Pontiac shuddering smoke on the shoulder of the road. When he saw the long, blond ponytail, he felt the twitching of his right foot on the accelerator.

"Libby Joyce can hitch a ride from someone else," Win said. "I'm sorry; I can't help it. I don't like her. She's exactly what's wrong with this town. She can wait for the next Good Samaritan."

He felt the seat beside him lighten. A loneliness returned that he had never noticed before because it had always been there.

"Jack, Jack," he muttered. "Don't leave just because of Libby Joyce."

And then, unbidden, he thought, What would Zoe's husband do?

Well, that was easy to answer.

Zoe would only marry the kind of man who would stop the car. Zoe would want her husband to offer Libby a ride—to the gas station or her own home, her choice. Zoe would expect her husband to turn the fins on the air vents so that the blast of cold would soothe the sweaty upper lip of the cow who owned the Little Lilac restaurant. Zoe herself would make small talk in this situation or, if Libby were in a complaining mood, would nod sympathetically.

He wasn't as good a husband as Jack would have been. Wasn't half the man Jack had been.

He drove by Libby's car, avoided meeting her sad cow eyes, and got fifty feet up the road before he put his foot on the brake.

He looked in the rearview mirror, half expecting to see his brother standing on the shoulder of the road instead of the husky restaurateur. Because he realized then that the soul of his brother was in every resident of Sugar Mountain—including, as hideous as the thought might be, Libby Joyce.

"Damn," he said.

The oath was as much directed at Zoe and his brother as it was directed at Libby. He shifted the car into reverse.

"Damn, damn, damn."

He backed up.

When he was parallel to the sweat-soaked restaurateur and her smoke-belching car, he pushed the passenger-side automatic window-opener.

Hot, tar-scented air slithered into the car, seeping into every heretofore cool crevice. He tasted tar with every syllable he uttered.

"Afternoon, Libby."

She stood mutely regarding him.

"You don't want a ride," he said, without looking at her. "Do you?"

Thirteen

Libby grimaced at him. He glanced at her, wondering why she hadn't answered immediately.

She wasn't any happier to see him than he was to see her. She looked toward town. He looked in the rearview mirror. There wasn't anybody else coming to help this damsel in distress. She looked ahead, down the long, lonely stretch of highway. No cavalry on its way, bugels blaring, rescue of damsels in mind.

He felt the prodding of his brother, just the slightest texture of feeling of a hand on the back of his neck.

"Pluh, pluh, pluh," he said.

Libby raised one side of her upper lip in a gesture expressing both puzzlement and contempt.

"Pluh, pluh, pluh," he said.

She jutted out her chin, brought her eyebrows together, seemed to be trying to shame him into getting a word out.

"Pluh, pluh, pluh," he said, each syllable more painful than the last. But the back of his neck was starting to hurt. The pressure was getting more insistent. Jack didn't have time to gently coax a little brother into being in love with a town. "Puhlease . . . get . . . in . . . the . . . car . . . and . . . let . . . me . . .help . . . you."

"Yeah, all right," she conceded, with all the grace of someone reluctantly doing a really big favor for someone.

She tried to open the passenger door which, although the lock button stood high and proud and open, stuck fast. She tugged. She groaned. She strained. She scowled at Win.

"Unlock the door."

"It is unlocked."

"If you don't want to give me a ride, just say so right now."

"I do want to give you a . . . well, actually I don't want to give you a ride. But that doesn't make the door lock."

"It won't open."

He leaned over, pushed the inside door handle. Nothing. He sighed. Put the car in neutral. Got out. Walked around the car and jiggled the door handle. Nothing. This was where having a brother who was a ghost, an angel, an apparition, or whatever should come in handy.

"Jack," he said. "Open the door."

He jerked the handle. Nothing.

"I'm not sure I want to get in a car with you," Libby said.

"Fine with me."

"No, wait. I'll do it. Nobody else coming."

"Jack, if you're so concerned about my giving this woman a ride, at least make it easy."

But it wasn't easy. He was standing in hell with a woman who smelled like blueberry pie and old socks and the door wouldn't open. He had had quite enough of the village of Sugar Mountain. He kicked the car. The door popped open.

"It's a very temperamental car," he explained, and walked around to the drivers' side.

She got in the car, hoisting a big leather purse and a plastic bag in which were stacked three pie tins. The space in the car felt diminished by tenfold—and the odor of pie and socks was overpowering.

Oh, Jack, he thought. *Charity that begins at home is probably what drives most runaways.*

"May I drop you off at your ranch?"

"Puh-puh-puh-lease," she said and he was oddly gratified that she had as much trouble with the word as he did. She was like him, in a way. And he could appreciate that. "Do you remember where it is? Oh, yeah, you tipped our cows one night."

"Did not," he said, his foot reaching instinctively to the brake so that he might throw her out of the car. Forget appreciate. "All right, well, maybe I did. But I was sixteen at the time."

"Still."

"All right, sorry. I had forgotten about it. I guess you're still mad."

"No, I'm not mad," she said, adjusting her weight as she slid the seat belt over her belly. "I'm just reminding you where I live."

He shrugged. She snorted.

"Jeeeeez, I'm just trying to do with right thing," he said, loud so that Jack—whether in the backseat or in heaven—could hear him. "I'm just talking about giving her son a father. That's all. I'm even willing to live in a town when I know Kurt is going to deliver my mail every morning and this woman here owns the only restaurant. And where Mayor Stern is going to be mayor—jeez, anybody who would willingly play Don Ho's best hits on a saxophone isn't fit for public office."

"Trumpet," Libby said. "He plays the trumpet. And you don't have to shout."

"I'm not talking to you!"

She looked at the backseat. Just a suit jacket. A crumpled-up scarlet-red dress. An empty water bottle.

"Pardon me for interrupting," she said.

"As I was saying," he said, and then he felt as if Jack were getting away from him. "I'm doing the right thing because I know you'd do the same for me."

"Oh, I don't know."

Win looked at her.

"Sorry," she said.

"And what I want to know is—" And now he knew he was practically shouting. "—WHY IS EVERYBODY MAKING IT SO HARD TO DO THE RIGHT THING?"

"You bring it on yourself."

He startled.

"What?"

"You bring it on yourself," Libby repeated. "Sorry, I was just going to tell you that folks don't think much of you because you don't think much of them. You think we're jerks—don't deny it—and you know what? We are. I'm a grumpy, grouchy restaurant owner whose feet hurt all day long. But anywhere you go in the world, Win, there's a woman just like me. Every small town, every big city has got 'em. And you know what? You're part of this town, even when you're gone. You can be a wanderer, but you'll always want to come home."

"Libby, here's your house. I wasn't actually posing that question to you."

"If you love yourself, you can love every person in Sugar Mountain—maybe not to the point where you want to kiss them or send them flowers, but enough so that you can make a commitment to live with them. If I could learn the same lesson, maybe I'd be a better person, too."

He stopped the car at the end of the gravel drive in front of a burgundy clapboard house. She opened the passenger-side door, letting all the cool air dissipate into the hideous heat. She put her leather purse on the ground and picked up her pies.

"You know what, Libby?" he said. "You're right. You're a grumpy, grouchy restaurant-owner, and just looking at the way your shoes fit, I'd suspect that your feet hurt all the time."

"And you're a last-chance guy who's going to die bitter and lonely when you're too old to hop up a mountain. But you're not going to do that, are you?"

He laughed. She did, too; and for a moment, just one moment, she looked . . . beautiful.

Then they remembered themselves.

"You wouldn't . . . no, you wouldn't want to come in and have some pie?"

He said, "You're right. I wouldn't."

"At least we understand each other."

And for one terrible second, they not only understood but also liked each other.

She seemed frankly relieved when he put his foot on the accelerator. He drove fifty feet before it became too uncomfortable.

"This is not easy, Jack," he said, though he couldn't feel his brother's presence at all.

He pulled a U and ploughed back into the billowy dust he had scraped up leaving Libby behind.

"Sure," he said. "Pie sounds great."

And he pulled the key from the ignition and stepped out into the flame-worthy heat.

He picked up her bags, waved to her husband, who appeared on the front porch, and followed Libby into the house.

Zoe said good night to the reverend, who glanced up from the first draft of his sermon and asked if she were going to be announcing her wedding in the upcoming Sunday bulletin.

"There is nothing to announce," she said firmly.

"Sorry, I must have misunderstood," the rever-

end said, and he truly meant it because there were
so many things in Sugar Mountain that confused
and baffled him that one more thing on that pile
of confusion and bafflement was, well, just one
more thing. "I don't know where I got that idea.
Maybe because you and Win were in that office of
yours so long and because he told everyone that
you were getting married. I must have misunderstood."

He took off his glasses. Looked at her with eyes
pinkened from fatigue. He would probably work on
the sermon until his wife retrieved him. He was the
only person Zoe knew who could say what he just
said and really mean it.

"Yes, well. It's not you who misunderstood. Have
a good evening."

The reverend jerked his head back up from his
sermon.

"Oh, yeah. You, too! See you tomorrow."

She cut through the sanctuary, rearranging a
vase of flowers on the table that featured the guest
book signed by the many relatives and house
guests who stayed in Sugar Mountain over a weekend. When she stepped out from the stone-cooled
air into the fiery oven of the late afternoon, a
familiar red car was parked at the curb. The passenger-side window slid down. She felt her lips
come together in a tight, prim line. His white
linen shirt was unwrinkled. His only concession to
the heat was a slight loosening of the knot on his
lavender-and-blue-checked silk tie.

"I gotta go shopping," Win said. "Would you go with me?"

"I'm not marrying you."

"Here, I'll turn down the air-conditioner. The sound must have made you misunderstand me. I said *shopping*. Not *marry*. Not as much commitment, takes place in a mall or a business district."

"Why do you need to shop?"

"Don't ask. But would you come with me?"

She leaned toward the window. The cool air was tempting. But then the memory of his kiss intruded.

"No, I can't," she said. "And besides, I thought we worked out this marriage thing. I'm not doing it."

"I'm not the one bringing up marriage. You are."

She pressed her lips together.

Guilty as charged.

"If I'm going to be living in Sugar Mountain, we're going to be seeing each other all the time, right?"

"What do you mean, *living*?"

"It's a very small town. The sign on the road leading out of town says two hundred fifty, and it said that eleven years ago. Probably includes cats, dogs, cows, and goldfish, too."

"You're not going to live here."

"Why wouldn't I?"

"Because you hate this place."

"Nah, it's not so bad. I told you, I can get used

to it. I have friends. At least, I hope you're one of them."

"Of course. I always have been."

"And I have to stay long enough to get to know my nephew Teddy. When does he get back from camp?"

"Tomorrow."

"I should at least stay long enough to get to know him. And then Paige is having another nephew of mine. Oh, and Kurt said that Kate has been looking peaked when he gives her the mail—in the morning. Think of all the baby presents I need to buy."

"Where were you thinking of going?"

"Breckenridge. We could have dinner there. They have real restaurants. I made a reserva—"

"Win Skylar, that sounds like a date!"

"Friends. Going shopping."

"I'll have to check on mom first."

"Is that different from checking with your mom?"

"Yes, there's a huge difference. It means I'm the responsible party. You'd have to promise . . ."

"No kisses," he said, crossing his fingers over his chest. "You said no more, and I respect that. I respected it eleven years ago when I had more hormones than the average teenage boy should be allowed. I'm respecting it now. I'm just going to wait until you ask me. And I'm warning you—I might not say yes the first time you ask."

She crossed her arms over her chest.

"But you aren't going to ask me," he concluded.

Then he smiled. Oh, that smile that broke down the strongest of feminine resistances.

"All right," Zoe said, and breathed in the temptingly cold air from the window. "All right. Shopping. Dinner. That's it."

She tugged at the door. Nothing.

"You have to unlock it."

"It is unlocked."

"No, really, I can't open it."

He put the car in neutral. Opened his door, walked around to her side. He leaned close; she smelled good. He eyed her lazily, the way he might regard a particularly luscious piece of fruit. The sleeve of his shirt, as it brushed against her arm, was cool and crisp and gave her goose bumps.

This was when it would happen, she thought. He'll kiss me again.

Then he'll start that marriage stuff again.

Such a one-track mind.

So aggravating.

Such a ridiculous notion, getting married.

So how was it she was disappointed when he tugged open the door and helped her into her seat without once trying to kiss her?

Fourteen

"I've heard that this man—" Mrs. Kinnear ogled Win over the tops of her bifocals. She placed a delicately hammer-like emphasis on the words *this man*. "This man has been all over town saying you're getting married."

"Mother, we're absolutely not. It's just he started talking to people and it's like the worst game of operator when you get three Sugar Mountain people in one . . ."

"Mrs. Kinnear, I really did want to marry your daughter."

Mrs. Kinnear placed a frail hand upon her frail chest, which enclosed a frail heart that could not bear much more than it had already been required to endure over the course of seven decades and change.

"So, it's true!"

"Oh, yes," Win said.

"Oh, no," Zoe said.

"Have you brought alcohol . . ."

"Mother, I think I'm not having another drink, but if I were, I'm old enough."

". . . cigarettes . . ."

"I hated the taste of them."

". . . pornography . . ."

"*Playgirl* is a bit over the top, I have to admit," Zoe agreed.

"I wasn't talking about *Playgirl*," Mrs. Kinnear said. She pulled the dog-eared copy of *Cosmo* out from a stack of educational *National Geographics*. "Sex Tips to Drive Him Wild? I was truly appalled when I read this."

"Mrs. Kinnear, I didn't bring those things into Sugar Mountain," Win said. "They were already here. Just go to the Shop'N'Stop."

"Teddy didn't come from the Shop'N'Stop. You brought him into her life."

"And what if he did?" Zoe asked wearily. "You love your grandson."

"I love him dearly. But I don't have to like Win because of it."

"That's too bad," Win said amiably. "Because I wanted to marry your daughter."

Mrs. Kinnear snorted.

"Sure, one of those put-up jobs where the reverend declares you man and wife and you go gallivanting who knows where, leaving Zoe to raise . . ."

"You're right. That wouldn't be fair to her."

"Oh, fine, so then you take her with you. I'd never see my daughter again. That's even worse."

"That wouldn't be fair to you or Teddy or anyone else in this town."

"So, you are talking about a real marriage?"

"In every sense of the word, that's what I was offering," Win said.

Mrs. Kinnear took off her glasses. "And with whom, I mean, where would you want to live?"

"I would never take Zoe away from this house, and I would have been honored to live in the same home as my mother-in-law. I don't take with this custom of shipping our elders off. You know, in certain Asian countries, the elderly are revered and honored as if they were gods."

Mrs. Kinnear sighed.

"That's as it should be."

"Ma'am, do you believe in forgiveness?"

"Of course," Mrs. Kinnear said tartly. "Young man, my husband Abraham Kinnear preached many fine sermons on the subject. Not that you would have ever heard them."

"But I think I understand him. When I ask for your forgiveness," Win said, "you have to give it to me."

Mrs. Kinnear wagged a finger at his face.

"Forgiveness does not come without repentance. You left my daughter alone to face motherhood."

"If I did do that, I repent."

Mrs. Kinnear put her glasses back on.

"Then, son—may I call you *son*?—I give you my blessing."

"MOTHER!"

"There's only one thing standing in the way of our wedding," Win said. "She said no."

Mrs. Kinnear's eyes widened.

"Zoe Kinnear, you say yes this instant!"

"You can't possibly mean that."

"Oh, yes, I do."

"You've never had a kind word for this man."

"I haven't had a kind word for him because he left you. Now that he's going to make you an honest woman and give Teddy a father, I think he's just dandy."

"You've lost your mind, Mother," Zoe warned.

"Maybe so, but in certain very sensible Asian countries, youngsters know to listen to their elders. As it is, I'll have to rely on his charm and good looks to sway you. Worked once, will work again."

"Thank you, ma'am, for your support," Win said. Mrs. Kinnear ground her chin into her chest. She had not been offering support.

"Ma'am, did you open your mail?" Win asked. "Kurt said you won a cruise."

"She's a semifinalist," Zoe said.

Mrs. Kinnear wagged her finger.

"No, this time I won it, fair and square. Four tickets for the *Sea Princess*. I could give two tickets to you for your honeymoon and keep two for me and Teddy."

"Heck of a honeymoon," Win said.

"Well," she sighed. "Teddy and I will have a wonderful time on a cruise."

"Mother, you're just a semifinalist. And as for you, Win, we aren't getting married."

"I'm sorry. I forgot. Not another word on the subject."

He made a zipping motion across his lips.

Zoe put her fingers to her temples.

"If you'd let your hair down, your head wouldn't hurt so much," he said.

She looked at him.

"There is nothing in that sentence that has anything to do with marriage," he said, adding slyly, "except, of course, if you take it that way."

She glared. He shrugged.

"I can see you are going to get along quite well," Mrs. Kinnear said. "Zoe, will you make me a tray to take to my bed? I think I could keep down some broth."

"I'll make you a tray," Win said. "Mother. May I call you *Mother?*"

Mrs. Kinnear winced as she rose from her comfortable armchair.

"Why don't you refer to me as *Mrs. Kinnear*—just for now. It seems to make my daughter nervous when you call me *Mother,*" she said. "No, no, Zoe, don't help me. I'm perfectly capable of getting up the stairs. Just get me that broth. I'm hardly up to any other food. Been such a shocking day. Well, maybe some of that chicken left over from last night, don't want to let it go to waste. And a small serving of potato salad. And green bean salad—the doctor said I must have my antioxidants. Oh, be sure to include a little sherbet. Cleanses the palate, you know. Shall I see you to the front door, Winfield?"

"I'll be taking Zoe with me."

"Oh, dear me. A date."

"Shopping."

She looked at him and winked.

"Gotcha, buddy. Will you bring her home at a decent hour?"

"You and I may differ on decent, but I'll have her home before dawn."

"See that you do, young man. When you're married, you may do as you please. Until then, please act with some decorum."

Zoe followed Win into the kitchen.

"Why'd you tell her that stuff about marrying me? A, I'm not marrying you. And B, you know darned well you're not Teddy's father."

He opened the refrigerator door.

"The truth is a very funny thing," he said, picking out a plastic container of potato salad and another of green beans. He laid them on the counter. "This afternoon, I went to the mayor's tavern with my brothers and I asked them what they would think if Jack were Teddy's father."

Zoe nearly dropped the plate she had pulled out from the top cabinet shelf. "What'd they say?"

"Well, neither of them would even admit the possibility. Besides the fact that nobody knew that you were seeing each other, Jack would never have taken advantage of a teenage girl. *Jack* would never have run out on his responsibilities. *Jack* would have always taken precautions. He was such a gentleman."

Zoe was silent.

"And if Jack found out he'd gotten you pregnant, he would have married you."

"I think so too," Zoe said quietly.

"But instead, the four Skylar brothers go up on

the mountains during a bad patch of December weather and there's a terrible accident."

Win paused; and when he spoke again it was much more softly.

"What would have been the harm of telling us, any of us, that Jack had a child on the way?"

"I didn't know until later."

"Then, later, whatever . . . it would have been a great comfort. Thinking of Jack living on through his son Teddy. But you didn't tell a single person, did you?"

"Well . . ."

"Who'd you tell?"

"I told only one person."

"Kate? Paige?"

She shook her head.

"The reverend?"

"No."

"There isn't anybody in this town who can keep a secret."

"You're right," she said carefully.

"Zoe, what is that noise?"

Zoe was grateful for the distraction.

"My mother's ringing a little bell she keeps on her nightstand. It means she wants that tray. Now."

"I don't have a nightstand bell, but would you hurry back all the same?" he asked as she trotted up the stairs with the tray.

The floral wallpaper in Mrs. Kinnear's bedroom had been purchased and pasted within months of her nuptials—the hydrangeas and morning glory pattern had long since faded to a sepia glow. The furniture was all curves and curlicues, with every available surface draped with antimacassars and doilies as if men with Brillcream were in the habit of breaking into homes and rubbing greasy heads on tender matrons' furnishings. The window air conditioner unit hummed wheezily. And, the pasha of all she surveyed, Mrs. Kinnear, lay on the double bed with a whisper-weight coverlet and sixteen pillows. On seeing Zoe, she laid down her copy of *The Collected Sermons of Abraham Kinnear.*

"Dear, that looks wonderful, but I was hoping I could persuade you to bring me a few pieces of bread. Maybe they would settle my stomach."

"Of course," Zoe murmured.

"And dear?"

"Yes, Mother?"

"I will be going to bed early. So, let's say good night now, shall we?"

Zoe put the tray on her mother's lap and kissed her forehead.

"I'll get that bread for you."

"And Zoe?"

"Yes, Mother?"

"I just want you to know that I always tried my best. Still do. It's just there's so many terrifying things in the world. So many ways that a child can take a wrong turn in life and never be able to find the path back home. I wanted to protect you from all that. Because I love you so much. So, maybe I was a little too strict with you. And then, when you had Teddy, I thought I had to stop you from continuing on a path that would . . ."

"I know."

"So, sometimes I've seemed like a real . . ."

And here Mrs. Kinnear quite unexpectedly used a word that was not part of her normal vocabulary. Because it rhymed with *hitch* and *switch* Zoe at first misunderstood. When she did understand, she was puzzled. For she had never, not once, thought of her mother as such.

"Mother, you're not."

"I hope not. But, Zoe, be careful with that man. Get him to the altar before you do anything you could regret."

"I'll be careful, Mother," she said.

"That's what I've always taught you. But I wish you would have listened to me earlier. It would have saved both of us a lot of heartache."

"I know, Mother. I know."

"If this doesn't work out, maybe you could call Rory Packer's mother? Just for me? She seems so very sad that her son didn't marry you. Maybe she'd feel better if you explained to her . . ."

"Mother, I can barely understand my life as it is. I don't think I could explain it to anyone else."

Fifteen

A date is defined sparingly, by *Webster's Dictionary*, as a social engagement between two persons which often has a romantic character. Its original publisher, Daniel Webster, didn't know about butterflies in the stomach, Dutch treat, rushing, game playing, barhopping, being stood up, padding one's autobiography, and remembering not to discuss one's ex at the dinner table.

Zoe was sure they were in a agreement that this was absolutely, positively not a date.

So, when he pulled the car out of the driveway onto Chestnut Avenue, they were not actually going on a date. It was not a date when they slipped through the quiet Sugar Mountain streets, passing houses as a kitchen light here and a reading light there blinked on. In some municipalities the completion of a workday would be considered sufficient reason to stay out late and consume alcohol and barbecued chicken wings dipped in blue cheese dressing in a noisy bar. But Mayor Stern's tavern was nearly empty and his neon sign sizzled for half a minute and died as it did every evening 'round sunset. Win and Zoe were on their own in Sugar Mountain's streets—except, of course, for teenagers, who were congregating at Stern's Folly Park so that they might skateboard and complain about the backwardness of the town, and their parents in particular.

Daniel Webster would have said this had all the earmarks of a date—he drove her to Breckenridge; he told her about exotic lands he had seen . . . the eastern coast of Africa, the punishing deserts of Arabia, the jungles of subtropical India. While she updated him on the past decade of her life, they ate a meal seated on a terrace over the Breckenridge Springs. When the first stirrings of the evening breeze came down from the mountains, he retrieved a jacket which he had tossed into the trunk along with his backpack. He slipped it on her shoulders and noticed that her trembling seemed more than just a chill.

If he weren't mistaken, there was the slightest touch of anger.

"What's the matter?" he asked, sitting down as the waitress laid two dessert plates in front of them.

Zoe waited until the waitress had retreated before she spoke. She leaned forward.

"I just want you to know this is not leading to marriage."

"We're two friends, out for a bite to eat and a little shopping."

She took a deep breath, bit her lip so hard she

tasted blood. And then said it all at once so that it would be said and over with.

"I just want to warn you that I'm not going to ask you to kiss me good night."

Win choked on his forkful of a diminutive pear tartlet.

"You think I'm going to ask you to kiss me."

"No," he said with as much *moi? absolument non!* as he could muster.

She crimsoned. A blush on a woman with her hair color was sometimes a little too much red in one place, what with freckles and all. Squelching the urge to duck her head or turn away, she tilted her chin up and kept her eyes firmly on his.

"I just don't want you to get the wrong idea. Just because we're in such a beautiful restaurant."

"Not at all."

"And just because we're having a wonderful time."

"Just friends. You have always been a good friend, Zoe."

He reached over to push an errant curl into the rigid bun, but he didn't do a good job of it and so she undid the clasp in her hair, tugged and fretted her curls to put it back up. But he took the clasp and shoved it into his shirt pocket. She froze, holding up her hair, until she realized how closely the pose resembled that of the "Beauty Tricks That'll Make Him Tick" column's model. She let her hair fall around her shoulders. A headache so low-level that she hadn't even noticed it was relieved.

"Zoe, I said we were just friends."

"But isn't all this just softening me up? Telling me you want to shop? Ha! Men don't shop."

"I want to get a pair of shoes. Girlfriends buy shoes together all the time. The world over. There's a shoe store in Annamanpour, highest city in Nepal, and it does a great business."

"You don't need shoes."

He bit his lip.

"You don't want shoes."

He looked down at his plate. "Yes, I do."

"Really? What kind of shoes are you looking for?"

"Comfortable but stylish," he muttered.

"You're impossible!"

"Zoe, I really want to buy a pair of shoes this evening. And as for kissing you, I won't lie. I'd love to. As for making love, I'm ready. Marriage? Sure. And the honeymoon—just you and me and the Lakeside delivery boy, with instructions to leave deliveries on the front porch."

She raised her eyes heavenward.

"But I said I wouldn't even kiss you until you asked me and I won't. Boy, if you put me through this much grief for having asked you to marry me once, I have to say that Rory must be a man of extremely hardy constitution."

"Just so we understand each other," she said coolly.

"Exactly what do we understand?"

"That I don't have any interest in kissing you."

"Fine. But I still plan on staying awhile. Maybe even living here."

"Win, you'd be miserable."

"Oh, it won't be so bad. Maybe I'll meet someone. Fall in love, marry, have kids. Hey, you could be my best man—although my brothers would feel slighted if you were. I'll have to ask my bride to have you be her maid of honor."

"There aren't many single women in Sugar Mountain."

"I'll have to ask the mayor for some tips on meeting women"

She bristled.

"You'd be bored. Sugar Mountain is boring."

"I'll get a job so I'll have something to do during the day when you're at the office. I'll see if Eckhardt's Hardware is hiring. Or maybe Libby Joyce needs a cook. Or I'll take over the abandoned photography studio. I've taken a lot of pictures in my travels. I think I know how to do it."

"Win, you're not staying."

"Then I'll have to not kiss you," he said, signaling for the check. "Because if I kiss you, we'll make love."

"We will not!"

He wagged his finger at her.

"If we make love, we'll get married. Get married . . ." He caught her disapproving look. "So, let's go shopping instead. The mall here is supposed to have everything. Sure you don't need anything at Victoria's Secret? I've never been anywhere in the world where they don't get the catalogues."

"No Victoria's Secret. And I'm still not asking you to kiss me."

"Fair enough."

After paying for dinner, Win put his arm around Zoe and guided her down the cobblestone walk to the Breckenridge Mall.

"They're closed, Win," she said smugly. "Just proves my point. This friendship thing was a ploy. You knew we weren't buying any shoes."

He stared at the 'sorry we missed you—please try again' sign hanging in the door of the shoe store at the mall entrance.

"How would I know when stores close?" He pointed to a pair of white lace-up rubber-soled shoes. "Do you like those?"

"Absolutely not," Zoe said. She stuck out her tongue.

"They're enough to make the person wearing them feel ugly and uncomfortable."

She nodded her agreement.

"And they won't fit you," she said. She pointed to the window on the other side of the door. "That's where the men's shoes are."

"Okay, mission unaccomplished," Win said, turning from the window. "I'll take you home."

After arriving at the car, he tried to unlock the door. The key didn't work. He kicked the door. It opened. He helped her into the passenger's side and came around to the driver's seat. Same problem. He kicked it. It opened.

"Have to take this into Fred's Auto Service," he grumbled when he put the key in the ignition.

"Win, what did you come back here for? I mean, why now, after ten years, did you have to take the money out of the Sports Shop?"

He looked at her speculatively. "You know about that, huh?"

"TJ told me."

He started the car.

"What do you need the money for?"

He drove out onto the highway.

"What do you think I need the money for?"

"Gambling debts?"

"Worse," he said, chuckling.

"You're being blackmailed?"

"Worse than that."

"Drug deal gone bad?"

"You've watched too many episodes of 'Unsolved Mysteries.' What if I told you I used the money to keep an orphanage from having to close its doors?"

He expected her laughter. Or at least an expression of disbelief. He expected her to say "yeah, right." Anyone else would have.

Instead, she smiled at him, a barely there lilt of her rosebud mouth, and it was the kind of admiring smile that he wished he got more often. Unfortunately, he had to keep his eye on the road, so he only caught a tantalizing touch of it.

"You're not kidding."

"I'm dead serious."

"All right. Where is it?"

"Thimphu."

"Never heard of it."

It was his turn to laugh.

"It's a town—well, come to think of it, it's just like Sugar Mountain. Except we're talking the mountains of Bhutan, not Colorado. They say the land is in the palm of God."

"The palm of God. That's beautiful. Sounds like how I feel about Sugar Mountain. Now, help me out. Where's Bhutan?"

"In the Himalayas, east of Nepal, south of Tibet. Thimphu is the capital and the prince lives in a castle carved into the mountain. Thimphu is bigger than Sugar Mountain, of course, but it's where I've done business for the past two years. It's a staging ground for Everest and the other climbs. There's a little foundling home near my favorite restaurant—I spent a lot of time in town between climbs. Sometimes I would stop in and talk to the Buddhist nuns who run the place," he said. He did not mention the repairs he had done for them when their roof collapsed. Didn't mention that when he was bored, he taught the kids American baseball. Didn't say anything about so many kids with no one to look out for them . . . except a group of Buddhist nuns and an American with a cynic's heart. He cleared his throat. Adjusted the rearview mirror that didn't need adjusting. "A few weeks ago, the nuns came to me because they were going belly-up. I said I'd see what I could do. They're kind of—" He talked now with his chin nearly tucked into his collar. "They're kind of relying on me to bail them out."

"That's really wonderful," she said, sighing.

He squirmed in his shirt, which had seemed to

be made of the softest cotton this morning but which now seemed like burrs woven into chiggers. Praise made him uncomfortable, always had.

"You'll find this interesting," he said. "My favorite restaurant is run by a lady very much like Libby Joyce. Same kind of—"

"I don't find that part interesting. I find it interesting that you would take on . . . Win, what's wrong?"

"Nothing. Nothing."

"What?"

He pulled over onto the shoulder of the road, overlooking a wheat field jointly owned by the Williams and Johnson families. He killed the engine, tried to open the door, and when it wouldn't work, hit the window with his fist. The door popped open.

"Hold on. I gotta make a phone call."

"Now?"

"Well, I want to catch someone in Bhutan before the day gets started."

"But it's late."

"Not where I'm calling."

He grabbed his suit jacket from the back seat and got out of the car. He reached in the breast pocket of the jacket, didn't find what he was looking for, and put the jacket on top of the hood. Then he walked around to the back of the car and opened the trunk. He took out his cell phone and dialed. Interspersed with an incomprehensible flow of syllables were the familiar words *FedEx, shoes, Sugar Mountain, Colorado* and *thank you.* He paced back and forth along the border of the weedy field, his path illuminated only by the full moon and the dancing fireflies.

It was at that moment that she felt the lightest pressure on the back of her neck, as if a hand were steadying her.

"Jack," she said softly. "Jack, please, leave me alone right now."

Persistent feeling of a hand caressing her own.

"Jack, I have a confession to make."

She tried hitting the window, just as Win had done when his door jammed. Except her fist was small and diminutive while his was large and calloused.

"Jack Skylar, you open this door right now."

She could feel him. And she didn't want to.

"Jack, I'm going to be very happy to have my life back the way it was before."

She noticed an odd smell, pungent like skunk and ominous like eggs left out in the sun for too long. It wasn't overpowering, but it made her all the more anxious to get out of the car.

"I'm going to paint watercolors and press flowers and ask Prudence Cruikshank if she wants help on the Women's Service Board. Because when he's gone . . ."

The door still didn't work. She hit the window again, this time hoping she'd get Win's attention. The smell was getting stronger.

"In fact, I think I hadn't been kissed in so long, by any male over the age of ten, that I just got a little off-kilter when he kissed me. Oh, Jack." She moaned piteously. "Oh, Jack, please, open the damn door. Because there isn't any reason to believe in you if you can't at least do something useful!"

Sixteen

The door burst open. She spilled out of the car. The gravel rubbed her hands raw. Win helped her to her feet.

"Jack!"

"You said *Jack.*" she said, wiping the dirt off the front of her skirt.

"No, I didn't."

"I heard you say *Jack.*"

"I must have said *thwack* or *smack,* which is the sound you made when you hit the ground."

He walked around to the trunk and threw the cell phone in. He slammed the lid.

"Or the sound that the trunk makes when it's closed," he added.

"You said *Jack.* You must believe in him."

"I don't have to believe in him. But I do believe that there is a hideous smell coming from this car," he said. He got up close to the passenger-side window, which was open just a tiny sliver. "*You* must have been b.s.-ing him."

"Huh?"

"Smell gets worse when you say something he doesn't like. I mean, if I believed in him, that's what I'd say."

"Okay." She took a deep breath and said loudly, "I'm not going to do watercolors and I won't press flowers and I'm not joining Prudence Cruikshank's service board."

"You don't have to shout at him."

"See, you do believe in him."

"Believing isn't getting us back in the car."

He tugged at the driver-side door handle. "All right, Jack, open up!"

"We have another problem besides this door," Zoe said. "It's that you don't believe in yourself."

He looked at her. Puh-leeze.

"No, really. I can't understand why you wouldn't be announcing to everyone what you were doing with the money. Have people think something better of you than that you have gambling debts or whatnot. And why you wouldn't want to go back to Thimphu right away to see what your money has done."

"Yeah, well, I'm not interested," he said, kicking the door. The door did not open.

"You must be a hero to them."

"I don't know," he said, going around to the passenger-side door. He kicked it. Hard. The full moon illuminated his expression of distaste.

"I think I figured it out," she said.

"Oh, yeah?"

He shoved his face up to the closed window of the passenger-side door.

"I think you don't want anyone in Thimphu to think of you as a nice guy. And you don't want anyone here getting the same idea. You don't believe in yourself."

"Uh-huh," he said absently. He straightened up. Kicked the door. Harder this time.

"I think you're uncomfortable if someone thinks highly of you. And so you're not going back to Thimphu; but if you got over that embarrassment about being caught in the act of doing something selfless—"

"Uh, Zoe, we gotta . . ."

"—you'd be more at peace with yourself. Believe in yourself, Win. And by the way, I want you to know how much I admire you."

". . . problem. Big problem."

"In fact, I feel all sweet on you," she said. "I think that smell is going away, by the way. Although maybe we can't smell it because we're outside the car."

"Well, we're going to stay that way," he said. "Outside the car. Because we're locked out."

"You're quite sure?"

With only the smallest quivering of moonlight, she could still see his mournful nod.

"Oh, but your keys."

"In the ignition."

"We can call Fred's on the cell phone."

"I just threw it back in the trunk."

"Can't you do that thing you do with the doors?"

"Okay, I'll try. But I don't think it's going to . . ."

He walked over to the trunk. Made a fist. Hit the trunk.

". . . work."

"JACK!" they both screamed.

Nothing.

"He's not here," Win said. "Or he's decided to leave us to our own devices."

"You know, he was the nicest guy. So steady. Chamber of Commerce material. And now that he's dead, he's a troublemaker. Just . . . just . . . just like . . ."

"Just like me?"

She glanced around the darkness. And shivered, from cold more than anything else.

He put his arms around her.

"I'm sorry we're locked out," he said. "But not sorry to be with you."

She laid her head on his shoulder. He caressed her softly scented curls. She didn't protest.

"You think he makes that smell in your car when someone's not speaking the truth?"

"Absolutely," Win said. "It happened to me this afternoon."

"Then would you do me a favor?"

"Okay."

He felt her chin graze his chest as she raised her head to him. Her lips were near his, her breath as soft as rain. He leaned back.

"I won't kiss you, Zoe, unless you ask."

"I'm asking."

"That's your favor?"

"I just have to know if I've been lying to myself."

He moaned as he pulled away from her helluva kiss.

"Zoe, if you want me to be the responsible one, you're going to have stop kissing me like . . . mmmmm, where'd you learn to do that, baby?"

He was referring to the way the pads of her fingers pressed against his chest.

"Instinct."

"Nature's a wonderful thing." He sighed. "But why are we doing this here and now?"

"Simple. We're in the middle of nowhere. We can't get into trouble. We can't even get back in the car. There's no one that's going to come by here tonight. This road is deserted."

"You're playing with fire."

She wagged her finger at him.

"I've got your number. You're a gentleman. Through and through. You aren't going to ask me to make love to you on a tar-and-gravel highway."

"Of course I wouldn't."

"And the mud and grass?"

"Okay, no, I wouldn't."

She pulled away from his embrace, reaching down to pick up the red dress and shook it out as if it were a piece of delicate laundry. The spangles and sparkles of the beads were like June bugs in the moonlight. She handed it to him.

"Let's go," she said, pointing to the distant hazy rim of light that was Sugar Mountain. "I think it's just under ten miles."

"Long walk."

"We don't have a choice. We can't possibly sit out here all night. Are you coming?"

He slowly picked up his jacket from the hood of the despicable car. Followed her from a distance that allowed him to keep her scent and see the barest outline of her form.

"Zoe, we're not going to walk all the way into town."

"You're supposed to be in better shape than me. So if I can do it, I don't see why you can't."

"Sure, but those shoes aren't such a good—" A sound that was something like a scream and something like a squeal made him sigh. "Oh, no!"

She had disappeared—swallowed up by the dirt at the side of the road. He sprang to action, pulling her out of a mud pit by the muddy scruff of her muddy neck. She had muddy hair, a muddy face, muddy arms, and if he could have peeked under her muddy dress, he was sure he would have found muddy legs. He helped her up to the shoulder of the road. His shirt was, of course, now muddy. Ruined, as well as he could tell in the moonlight.

There was the distinct aroma of cow pies and tar. An owl hooted. Overhead, a jet glided serenely across the moon.

"As I was saying, those shoes are sensible enough for the office or for being in town but not for . . ." He caught her glare, even if her eyes were completely and utterly surrounded by mud. She swiped a finger across her cheek and shook off the excess. Did the other cheek. It was not much of an improvement. He sniffed. "Is that where the ranchers bring their cows to drink?"

"It was, until we didn't get any rain. Now it's just a ditch. We're just going to have to keep walking." She put her weight down on one bare foot. *"Oh!"*

"I think you twisted it. You're certainly not going to make it ten miles."

"Do you have any suggestions?"

"I can carry you. On my back."

"I weigh too much."

"What are you? One-twenty, one-thirty, tops? I once carried a Sherpa guide with a broken leg down the southern slope of Everest. He had the broken leg. Not me."

"How long will ten miles take?"

"Two, two-and-a-half hours."

"My mother will still be up. She likes the late show."

"So?"

"Mrs. McGillicuddy will be up. She doesn't have air-conditioning. Likes to sit out on her front porch. And yet, if we don't get home until morning . . ."

"I think I see where this is going. Why don't you leave it to me? Just trust me on this; your reputation is not going to have the slightest blemish on it. Get on my back."

He crouched down and she put her arms around his neck. He hoisted her legs up around his hips.

"Town's back that way," she said.

"Remember to trust me."

He carried her with as little effort as he would a baby.

"Winfield Skylar, where are we going?"

"Luckily, there's a place to freshen up."

He carried her up the path, through the trees, past the clearing where just three days before she had sat with her paints and her unclaimed passions. He followed a trail that was nothing more than a subtle bend in the direction of the Solomon's seal leaves and the branches of the conifers.

"This is where you were walking to just the other day."

She felt rather than saw his nod.

He set her in a densely grown pocket next to a rocky crag and from beneath it pulled a Davy Sparks lantern—the kind miners of the previous generation would have found familiar. Holding aloft the golden glow, Win illuminated the mouth of a cave.

Growing up in what had a century before been a silver-mining town, Zoe had played with her friends in abandoned mines and shafts of half-completed strike dreams. But this was nature's work, and she stared in awe at the stalactites, which formed a ceiling more beautiful than any basilica. Rivulets of copper, quartz, and silver sediment sparkled more intensely as Win lit three Coleman lanterns he had stored here.

Only when the cave was fully lit did she see the beautiful, wondrous pond of black, still water.

"Some people have temples, churches, holy

places," Win said. "This is mine. Found it just a year before I left home. Isn't it beautiful?"

"Oh, yes."

She looked down at herself, the contrast filling her with embarrassment. To say nothing of revulsion for the cattle smell.

"If you want to take off your clothes, I promise I won't look."

"But what will I wear when I wash up?"

He held up the red dress.

"There's also my suit jacket. I can get you back home in two-and-a-half hours and you'll look a little scandalous, but at least, you won't smell as bad and you'll be home."

"Deal."

He laid the dress down at the edge of the pond and retreated to the mouth of the cave. She pulled her dress halfway over her shoulders.

"Uh, Win?"

"Yeah?"

"How deep is the water?"

"Two or three hundred feet."

She slipped the dress back into place. Considered the placid surface of the pond.

"This isn't going to work."

He came back into the cave. He had taken off his shirt. Her mouth went dry.

"Why not?" he asked.

There were a hundred reasons why this wasn't going to work, starting with the fact that his skin was the color of caramel and looked as if it needed to be kissed. But she only said, "I'm the sort of girl who swims in YMCA or motel pools. If you can't paint the bottom of this thing light blue, I don't want to get in."

"Let me help you."

He went to the other end of the pond where, surprisingly, he pulled a wooden crate out from behind a rock. From inside he pulled out a large plastic sheet, which he shoved away, and a white, fluffy bath towel. He brought the towel to her.

"Take off your dress."

It seemed silly and petulant to argue.

"Just promise you're going to get me home."

"I'm going to carry you every step of the way."

"As soon as we get cleaned up?"

"The very moment."

She pulled her dress up over her shoulders and let it drop to the floor of the cave.

Seventeen

This would have been an excellent time for her to have worn matching underwear. Even her mother said matching underwear was important in case of car accidents and other mishaps involving paramedics and emergency room personnel who might be inclined to provide lower quality care based on whether one's undies declared one to be a lady. But doing laundry for three people was tough enough without having to safety-pin bras and panties together so they'd make it out of the dryer and onto her body at the same time.

She wore a denim blue cotton bra and a white lace tap pant. The left strap of the bra was pinned together because she kept forgetting to sew it up. But she didn't get the feeling Win minded that her undies didn't match and they weren't from a catalog.

She was a little self-conscious as she stood up because there was, of course, her stomach. Before she had Teddy, her stomach had been flat and smooth. Now, although she did abdominal crunches (ten, once a week, whether she needed it or not, if she remembered), her stomach was rounded. And there was the slightest crisscross of pale stretch marks up and down the sides of her belly. But his gaze was all admiration. She had to remember that she was wearing more fabric than could be found on most bathing suits.

And that sex goddesses aren't ordinarily caked in mud.

He slipped off his shoes, tugged on his belt.

"I don't have a dryer here," he said. "So there's no way I can dry those things if you get in the water that way."

"You go in first."

He turned away, pulled down his pants. She giggled.

"What?"

"Mrs. McGillicuddy's right. You have a tight butt."

He took off his pants and slid into the water. Treading lightly, he found footing on a crevice.

"All right, your turn."

He raised his face, closing his eyes. She took off bra and panties. Undid her hair. Carefully, she slipped into the water. It was cold and smelled like a blue popsicle. She ducked her head under, feeling the water wash through her hair, slither up her body. She instinctively reached for a bottom, found none, and started to panic. He pulled her up to him.

"You look like a mermaid," he said. "I love the way the water clings to your lashes like diamonds."

She cleared her throat.

"I just want to get washed up."

"Of course. Here, let me help you with your hair."

She clung to him while he squeezed water and mud out of her hair. Then he pulled her under and she shook her hair out. On the surface, he squeezed her hair again. After several repetitions, her hair was shiny and fresh-smelling. Her smooth legs brushed against his muscular thighs. Her breasts swelled on the water's surface and her nipples hardened. He wiped away the mud on her neck.

"In Japan, they say the sexiest part of a woman's body is the nape of her neck," Win said lazily, parting her hair so that he might kiss the smooth hairline. Virgin skin there, touched only by a starched-and-ironed collar or the tines of a comb as she put up her hair in the morning. His kiss made her knees draw up, up, up so that she was holding him, squeezing him.

"I think I'm clean now," she said raggedly.

"Then let's get out."

He helped her find purchase and get out of the water. Following behind, he brought the towel up around her and dried her hair. He found a comb in his pants pocket and offered it to her. She put the towel around herself and tucked it together atop her breasts. While she combed her hair, he smoothed out the plastic sheet and popped the air, filled it up quickly to make a soft mattress. This he covered with a thin, blue blanket—*pashmina*, he would later explain—and then he stepped out of the cave to grab a handful of blooms from the climbing wood anemone.

He scattered yellow blossoms on the bed he had made. The scent was not unlike the first day of a rose's opening.

"This is my altar," he said, lifting the wet curls from her shoulders.

"And you, Zoe, you are who I worship."

A shiver went through her, not from cold or fear or even his touch. Just his words unleashed a craving for something that she couldn't even name, for she had never truly had it, for something she had missed in a life with only two wishes. When he finally—it seemed to be forever between his words and his actions—when he finally kissed her, she felt flame course through her. Shivers gone, replaced by raw heat. She dropped the comb and it went *ker-plunk* in the pond and then disappeared. She wanted him inside her, filling all the hollow parts of herself, touching all the places that cried out to be touched, holding her and bringing her to . . . well, what? Because she did not even know how wanting and yearning could—should—be satisfied.

"Win, make love to me now," she said.

"Let's take our time," he said. "And if you change your mind . . ."

"I'm not going to change my mind," she cried. "I want you as much, if not more, than you want me."

She pulled out of his embrace, as enticing as it was, and sauntered over to the flower-strewn bed,

fully aware of his appraising eye. And the mark of
his desire, the raw hardness of his manhood.

Coursing through her was a delicious sense of
feminine power—all the better since his kisses had
the power to make her throw away all that was right
and proper. After all, having sex outside of marriage, purely for pleasure's sake . . . but who was
she kidding? She did love him, had always loved
him, even if she hadn't admitted it. Because loving
a man like Win—who now stood, arms crossed over
his chest, chin tilted so that his dimple was at best
advantage—loving Win was a risk. His name would
never be said in an approving manner in the same
sentence as *respectable*. And she was a woman who
had avoided risks and liked the word *respectable*.

She couldn't have said where she'd learned what
she did next. In fact, it was the sort of thing a
woman only learns by doing. This was her first try.
But she wanted him. And every woman knows, deep
in her heart, how to get a man.

She paced just a few steps one way and then a
few steps another, as if she were modeling the latest
in towel wear. Or giving him a private dance. Then
carefully she tugged at one end of the towel.

She was actually a quite modest woman. In high
school, when the other girls yanked off their
clothes in the locker room and charged through
the showers, she had had a tendency to perform
topographic miracles so that the towel would drop
from her body just about the moment she was but-
toning her last button at her collar. When she was
at home, she seldom looked in the mirror for any-

thing other than a spinach-between-teeth or a gee-don't-my-hips-look-fat appraisal. And she was only too aware, when putting on jeans fresh out of the dryer, that she had a few more curves every year.

All of which added up to: She was no exhibitionist; but here she was, in the dark glow of the cave, performing a striptease to the *chig-chig-chig* of the dragonflies and oh, Win couldn't take his eyes off of her!

When she lay down, she was surprised that the camper's gear was as soft as a featherbed. The crushed anemones released an undernote of musk that complemented the rose smell.

He looked dazed and that was exactly what she wanted. He looked awed and that was exactly what surprised and delighted her. He looked strong, powerful, and sure of his masculine self when he strode to the bed.

"Zoe, glorious Zoe." He sighed, standing above her; then, after several excruciating seconds in which she feared he might be responsible enough for the both of them, he dropped to his knees. She lay beneath him, reveling in the feeling of surrender.

"I brought something with me," he said.

He tugged away, found his pants, and pulled from his back pocket a crinkly plastic package.

"I hope you don't think I was planning this all along," he said.

"Did you?"

"Well, not exactly this way."

She noted the hesitation. Then decided it didn't matter.

"Then I'll have to be glad about fate."

She bucked against him as he knelt between her legs.

"No, no, not yet." He trailed his fingers down from her collarbone, across the valley between her breasts; and then, dreamily he caressed each breast.

"But I've waited so long."

He pressed his hand against her belly—not too round, and yet not flat—and then as his hand grazed the pale copper hair of her womanhood, she gasped.

"Win, I don't think I can . . . wait," she said, and at that moment she had to hold his hand steady for he would have retreated and she couldn't have borne that—for when he touched her, it was as if she stumbled and, once stumbling, did not right herself. Instead, holding his gaze as her guide, she felt the first, concentric spasms of her ecstasy. In that moment, as the rush of sensation made her eyes flutter closed, he brought her into the true realm of the senses.

When she had somewhat—and it could only be somewhat—composed herself, she opened her eyes. He stared at her thoughtfully.

"So, that's what all the fuss is about?"

He laughed.

"Yes, that's a little bit of what all the fuss is about."

He lay next to her and put his hand behind his head.

"But aren't you going to make love to me properly?"

He smiled like a lazy lion.

"I didn't know you'd want more."

"Oh, but I do," she said. She sat up, for a moment hesitating out of embarrassment.

"What's wrong?"

"I'm so wet."

"Darling, that's what's going to make this wonderful," he said, and he pulled her to him so that she straddled him. He tugged the condom out of its packet.

"Here, let me," she said.

It wasn't the easiest thing to learn; but on the other hand, she'd learned to ride a bicycle without training wheels when she was six, learned to pump her own gas when Fred's Gas Station had to cut back on workers, and learned the Texas Two-Step at one of Barbara Martin's New Year's Eve parties. Win nodded his approval when she had finished.

He made a sound somewhere between a sigh and a groan when she guided him into her. When he was inside her, he filled her, completed her; and as she moved against him, at first only for his pleasure but soon enough for hers, she felt herself being tugged toward the shore of a distant land—a nation of two, a kingdom they ruled.

"Hey, don't fall asleep," Win said later, much later. "I gotta get you home—or those Sugar Mountain tongues will be wagging."

"It's all right."

"No, it's not. It's already two o'clock in the morning. Miss Zoe Kinnear does not come home that late."

"People shouldn't be so judgmental," she said sleepily.

"Oh, no?"

"They should mind their own beeswax."

"Zoe, wake up."

"There's plenty of people in Sugar Mountain who stay out late. There's a double standard here because I'm a minister's daughter and I'm the church secretary."

"You do understand we're going to have to marry to salvage your tattered reputation?"

"Oh, fine, fine, I'll marry you, but just let's do something illicit one more time."

Much later, she awoke, blinking at the lamplight.

"Win, isn't it wonderful that those lamps kept dry enough to use for—what? twelve years?"

"Uh, well, actually—"

"And this mattress—every year I have to buy Teddy a new sleeping bag and inflatable mattress for boy scouts because they get moldy."

"Uh, well, actually—"

"It's so magical."

"Uh, well, actually—"

"Actually what?"

"I brought everything over here just yesterday, before I picked you up from work. You don't mind, do you, darling? . . . uh, darling?"

Eighteen

"You're mad at me."

"Darn right I am."

"For what?"

"For that!"

Wearing the scarlet spangled dress that barely, just barely covered the lace border of her panties, Zoe pointed indignantly at the vista lit with motherly generosity by the morning sun. He glanced at the sun and then lowered his eyes. But that was no remorseful expression on his face. She tugged down hard on her dress. Picked up one shoe. Put it on. Looked for the other. Remembered that it was out there—on the road. She charged into the dew-kissed morning.

"You're mad at me because the sun came up?"

"No. Yes. No. Yes. Just get me home, Win."

Win was an agile man, quick to respond to an emergency, but all his rapid-fire responses left him still trailing twenty feet behind her—his pants unbuttoned at his hips, his shoes untied, his suit jacket slung across his bare shoulder. He buckled his watch with his teeth, a feat which would have impressed her had she turned, even once, to observe him. Instead, every tree she slammed past resulted in an unceremonious slap on his face by a spruce or juniper branch. And after each slap, he'd get a quick gander of sashaying bugle beads and white lace. He'd be off and running.

"How's your ankle?"

"Just dandy."

"I thought you liked . . . what we did."

"I did. That's the whole point."

"And when we're married, we can do that every night."

She stopped. Turned around. He nearly tackled her—accidentally of course. Her breasts heaved up and almost out of the low, satin-trimmed neckline. Her skin was creamy white, dusted with a few piquant freckles. She quivered and shivered with anger—and the unintended effect was not unlike what he had seen with Hong Kong go-go dancers. He stared hungrily, thinking of how those breasts had been his to caress just hours before—and then he looked up at her face.

Her expression was a mixture of furious and more furious.

"You tricked me into saying yes to your proposal."

"How?"

"By making love to me."

"You asked me. Twice."

She made a sound somewhat like that of a bear. A livid bear.

And then she charged away. A spruce branch reached out and gave him a *thwack!*

"Maybe Matt's right," he mused, rubbing his cheek. "Maybe women are from Mars. Zoe! Zoe! Hold up. What you're upset about, I think, is that I planned to make love to you."

"That's just part of it," she threw over her shoulder, along with a word that sounded like *smirk* or *dirk*.

"At a certain point I was hoping—okay, *scheming* if you want to use the word—to get you to the cave yesterday evening so that I could make love to you and then ask you, again, to marry me."

"Is that where you've taken other woman?"

"No, actually, you're the first." *And the last,* he thought. "What I mean is, I'm not the kind of guy who can hold hands for four years. I'm not like Rory Packer."

He nearly ran into her because she stopped unexpectedly on the trail and shoved her finger at his face.

"Rory Packer is a good man."

"He's not what makes your heart go pitter-pitter-patter. Or any other part of your body."

She whirled and charged. A chipmunk scampered across the path; a squirrel dodged her feet.

"I didn't make the car lock," Win said. "I didn't fall in the mud. I was prepared to piggyback you all the way to—"

"But you stopped to use the phone. Conveniently near your little love shack."

"I needed to make a phone call."

"Why?"

"You wouldn't believe me if I told you."

"Try me."

"I was calling Bhutan. Getting a pair of really comfortable shoes shipped over for Libby Joyce. The same pair the restaurateur I know has. Libby's feet hurt something awful when she's on 'em all day and I wanted to do something about it."

He hung his head. Was there really anything so wrong about wanting to help out a neighbor? he seemed to be asking.

She stared at him.

"You are one pitiful liar."

"No, I'm one pitiful truth-teller."

"You hate Libby Joyce."

"*Hate* is such a strong word. She's hard to get to know, but she's okay. And she actually persuaded me to abandon my first plan, which was to lure you to the cave and make love to you."

"But that's what you did."

"No, what I did was my second plan—which was to court you. Taking you to dinner was supposed to be part of that."

"And the other part."

"Being a nice, friendly guy. Have you fall in love with me. Slowly, if necessary. I didn't talk it over with her or anything. It's just that when I spent some time with her, I realized I could be part of this town. So plan B was to woo you, fair and square."

"You still made love to me. That's plan A."

"Loved every moment of it."

She bristled. Her bugle beads twinkled like dewdrops on a mulberry bush.

"Look. I admit it: I thought if you made love to me, you're just old-fashioned enough to think it was like making a lifelong commitment. You're the kind of woman who thinks you don't make love to a man unless—" He stopped abruptly. "Oh, Zoe, I've got your number. You don't love Jack."

She swallowed.

"What do you mean?"

"You don't *love* Jack. You feel loyal to him. That's what it is—loyalty. Lifelong loyalty. Affection, sure. Missing him, absolutely. But that ain't love. What we got between us is love."

"It is not," she squawked.

"You're one pitiful liar, baby. This is bigger than loyalty, bigger than mutual affection and courtesy and shared interests. It's love, baby, bigger than Godzilla and just as scary."

"I'm not scared," she said, tilting her chin up. "I'm not scared at all."

"You don't have to be, because I love you, too. I always have. I needed to grow up, to leave this town, but I'm ready to come back. And be your husband."

She narrowed her eyes, brought her face up close to his.

"I'm not going to mah-mah-mah . . ."

"You can't say it," he said, grinning. "You're such an old-fashioned—"

She closed her eyes. Thought of Rory Packer.

"I'm not going to marry you."

She whirled and charged into the brush.

He scratched his head, puzzled.

Then she screamed.

He ran further on the trail to find her, stately and yet trembling, at the clearing. No more than ten feet before them was the bright red car, a twinkling of sunlight reflecting off its hood, which was raised as if in salute to them.

But it wasn't the car that was of interest to Zoe, who tugged and pulled at her dress until she realized every inch she covered of her thighs meant less to cover her bosom.

The car wasn't all that interesting to Win, who with a mournful sigh swiped his back pocket and realized that his shirt was back there, somewhere, muddy and smelly and on the floor of the cave.

No, it wasn't the cheerful red sports car that captured their attention and horror. Rather it was the beaten-up, dark blue tow truck that was parked directly in front of the vehicle on the road's shoulder. The dark blue tow truck with the words *Fred's Auto Service* and the establishment's phone number painted in white on its passenger-side door. A squat, bald man wearing a pair of precisely pressed coveralls not yet stained with the day's labors came out from under the hood of the car. When he slammed shut said hood, he saw the couple.

At first he stared, silently, seeming to take particular note of the absence of Zoe's shoes. His head bowed in contemplation of this matter, Fred (identity confirmed by the cheerily embroidered name patch over his left breast pocket, as if Zoe hadn't had her own car serviced by his establishment for the past ten years and Win hadn't once dated his daughter)—Fred muttered that someone had called in this morning that there was an abandoned vehicle on the shoulder of the road.

"But it don't look like there's anything wrong with it 'cept you're down a pint of oil and you need some windshield-wiper fluid," Fred said. From beneath thick eyebrows he hazarded a glance at Zoe's dress. The sun bounced red and silver speckles of color off her dress and onto his weathered face.

"All right, you can figure this out. We spent the night together," Zoe blurted.

Fred took a shirt out from the back pocket of his coveralls. His wife had declared the shirt unfit for wearing and so it was his dipstick-wiper and sweaty-forehead blotter.

"The car doors don't work," Zoe said.

Yeah, sure, Fred thought, with a subtle lift of the corner of his mouth.

"Besides, we're adults and we're allowed to do what we want," Zoe added. "He asked me to marry him."

Fred spit tobacco juice out the side of his mouth.

"Look, I hope you don't mind, but I don't care what you did and who you did it with and why you did it in the first place. I just care about whether

I gotta tow a car. And I don't. Because the car is just fine. Nothin' wrong with it."

He reached out and opened the passenger-side door. With perfect courtesy he helped her get in, averting his eyes when more of her panties popped out from under her hem. He handed her one muddy shoe which he had found on the road.

"Most men use the run-out-of-gas story. Just tell me he didn't force you."

"No, no, he didn't."

"Good. Then that's the end of the matter, far as I'm concerned."

"You're not going to tell anybody?"

"I'm no gossip."

"Thank you," Zoe said.

"If you want to thank me," Fred said, and here he snarled, narrow-eyed and pugnacious, at Win, "put some windshield-wiper fluid in that thing. And a can of oil. Maintaining a vehicle is as important as feeding your children."

"I don't get how that door could open," Win said.

"Yeah, sure," Fred said. "Let's try this one."

He walked around the car and popped open the driver-side door without any apparent difficulty.

"Are you driving her home?"

Win nodded.

"I'll wait 'til you get the car started. Just you be glad she isn't *my* daughter."

Fred got in the tow truck.

"Get me home, Win," Zoe said. "My mother gets

up at seven o'clock. She can't make her own breakfast and . . ."

There was a certain way that she tucked her hair
into a ponytail that left no doubt—take me home,
buster.

He looked back once at the trail, at the beauty
she seemed to reject.

"I can't face this again," she said. "The gossip,
the talking behind my back, the snide remarks, the
bad feelings."

"People in Sugar Mountain love you. I'm the one
they're going to blame. They'll think I led you
astray."

"But you're leaving. You don't have to listen to
them."

"I'm not leaving," he said.

He turned the ignition.

"Zoe, you act as if people 'round here don't have
anything better to do than gossip."

"They don't."

"They have their own lives, and another thing—
times have changed. Sugar Mountain's changed—at
least a little bit. They aren't as judgmental as they
used to be. They're good people; they're try-hard
kind of people. Oh, listen to me. I've fallen in love
with them. They're absolutely nice people who are
just worried about you. Even Fred, here, he just
doesn't want your feelings hurt."

He tugged at his pocket, looking for his key, and
then remembered that he had left it in the ignition
the night before.

"Zoe, you don't need to worry about them."

She bit her lip.

"Just drive me home."

"You don't need to worry about whether the Cruikshank sisters titter and twitter. They will. You don't need to fret about whether your mother's bridge club yaks it up about you. They will. You're going to walk into the Little Lilac and Libby Joyce is going to stare at you. You're a brave woman, a good woman, and you know that."

"Drive me home," she said tightly.

"And the reward for marrying a bad boy like me is going to be heaven and more heaven every time you get into bed with me."

Her eyes narrowed.

"Drive me home."

"You're going to marry me, baby."

"Drive."

"You're going to marry me and in, oh, about a decade or so, talk'll die down. You couldn't have stood it when you were younger but you've grown up. Been through some things. Done some maturing. You'll stand the talk."

"Just drive me home."

He turned the ignition. Nothing happened.

"Wonder if Fred did something to the car," he said.

Tried again. Nothing.

"I'm going to go talk to him."

He pulled at the door handle. Nothing.

"It was working just a second ago," Zoe said, only momentarily distracted from her pique.

"It's not working now."

He pounded on the window. Nothing.

And then, with a great cry of frustration, he put his hand on the horn until Fred got out of his truck and sauntered back to their car to see what was the matter.

"We're locked in," Win said.

"What?" Fred mouthed.

"We're locked in," Win said, louder and more expressively.

Fred leaned close so that his lips nearly touched the glass, leaving a thin smudge of condensation with each word he spoke.

"Try the door," Fred said.

"WON'T WORK!"

Fred tugged on the door latch. Pulled. Pushed. Said a few words his missus would have been surprised to hear him say. Shrugged.

"I'll tow ya!"

"Oh, no," Zoe said. She yanked at the door, shoved, pushed, jammed, wiggled, jiggled—somehow thinking that the force of her personality and character, just plain determination, would let her out of the car.

Fred sauntered to the tow, backed it up, and got out again, pulling the hook down to meet the fender of the car.

"I've got only two questions for you," Win said.

"What?" she asked, annoyed. She pounded the window. Nothing.

"Are you going to marry me and would you like to wear my jacket?"

She wasn't going to answer the first, but the second question gave her some pause. Tough call as to whether it was worse to be towed into town wearing a scanty guest towel's worth of scarlet or riding shotgun next to a half-naked hunk.

Nineteen

Men who make their living in the vehicular industries fall into either of two categories. Those who are reckless and those who develop a surplus of respect for the inherent risks of travel.

Fred was in the latter category. In fact, he was something of a leader in the other category. Slow, methodical in his driving, he never pushed the speed limit, always came to a fully measured and somewhat leisurely stop at each intersection, and tended to drive with his head darting this way and that—one never knew when a car, meteorite, UFO, or tornado might run smack into one's path.

So it was that at seven o'clock in the morning, Fred led the slowest and shortest of parades down Chestnut Avenue. One tow truck pulling one red car.

But this parade did not lack for observers. In fact, the mayor—if he had not at that very moment been counting the champagne bottles stored beneath his bed—would have been jealous because the Fourth of July parade should be so well-at-tended. Folks on their way to work, farmers on their way to Eckhardt's Hardware Store or the Little Lilac for a spot of early morning coffee, and everyone who got the paper delivered—they all stood on the sidewalk eyeballing Win and Zoe, seated at a forty-five degree angle to each other. Some people waved, apparently confusing a mid-August morning of no particular merit with the birthday of our fair republic and the stately progress of the tow truck with the festooned floats the building of which Mayor Stern personally supervised.

"I'm not marrying you."

"Jack is making a mighty powerful smell."

Mrs. Johnson, wearing a powder blue bathrobe, waved her Sugar Mountain *Chronicle*.

"I'm still not—eeeeuwww." Zoe popped open the glove compartment. Took the cardboard cutout of a pine tree and put it up to her nostrils. Sniffed mightily. "There's a rational mechanical explanation for this."

"I'm sure there is. The carburator intake valve's misconnected. Positive you don't want my jacket?"

"No. Look, I don't love you."

Win tucked his face into his jacket.

"That's fine." He grimaced.

"I might have had lust for you."

"Uh-huh. You're making the smell worse."

She sniffed the pine tree. Coughed. Looked out the window. Waved to the woman who owned the bakery before realizing that when she waved, the little patch of scarlet fabric slid down.

"I've got an idea," Win said. "Just repeat after me. *I love you, Win.*"

"Are you out of your . . ." She felt a heaving sensation. What was left of her dinner was going to make an appearance if the smell didn't get any better. "All right. I love you, Win. But your brother Jack was a better man. Responsible and mature."

They were one block shy of Fred's Auto Service. The staff of Lakeside Foods stood as a group, staring solemnly. The librarian, who had had an otherwise ordinary walk to work, peered into the car on the driver's side and his facial expression alternated rapidly between a scowl and an appreciative gander at Zoe. Mr. Eckhardt and his assistants spilled out onto the sidewalk. Zoe pulled and tugged at the neckline of the scarlet dress, but there was only so far that the fabric would go.

"Your brother Jack was a better man," she repeated. "Responsible and mature."

"He was older, more settled," Win said. "Respectable."

"He was older, more . . . you know, you're right. He was older and more settled. Much more respectable than you'll ever be."

"But it was me—I mean, Win—I mean—*you* I loved . . . oh, heck, I was . . . I was . . ."

"IN LOVE WITH YOU ALL ALONG," the two of them said together.

They stared at each other for a good long time, nearly immune to the blandishments of the ladies from the flower shop who pointed and waved from their sidewalk perch.

And suddenly, in a way that Fred would have been hard-pressed to explain in mechanical terms, the interior of the car began to smell like the first tender bloom of lily of the valley. *Carburator intake valve must've fixed itself,* Fred would have said.

"I love you, Zoe," Win said.

"It's true," she said. "I love you, too."

"Darling, you don't have to cry about it."

"Yes, I do, because I never wanted to be in love with someone who would make me parade down Chestnut Avenue in a showgirl's dress."

"Look on the bright side. Think how much everyone'll have to talk about."

He kissed her and didn't stop kissing her when Fred stopped the tow in front of his shop. Didn't stop kissing her when Fred hoisted himself out of the driver-side door and signaled that he was going to get the crowbar to get them out. Didn't stop kissing her when Fred stood for several minutes staring, baffled and confused. Didn't stop kissing her when Fred hooked the car back to the tow and pulled truck and car into the three-station garage where he performed his best work.

Fred closed the garage doors. Walked into the office. Locked up the register and the cash box. Gave his assistant a fifty-dollar bill and told him to take the day off. Wrote *out of order* on three pieces of paper and taped them to the pumps.

And then Fred combed his hair back with a little Brillcream, spritzed himself with Hai Karate, and walked home to visit with the missus.

"I was thinking of a small wedding," Win said

later that morning when they had untangled their limbs. "Just as long as it's quick. Tomorrow's soon enough."

She tugged at the door handle and was surprised when it opened. Then she fell out onto the grease-covered floor of the auto repair shop.

"Is that a yes?" Win asked, peering out the driver-side window.

"I got a call this morning," Mrs. Kinnear said when Zoe brought her the breakfast tray. Mrs. Kinnear smoothed the folds of her bed jacket. "It was from Mrs. McGillicuddy."

"Is she going to be able to make it to the bridge club today?"

"That isn't what she was calling about."

"Well, it's awfully early to be making phone calls."

"Zoe, it's ten-thirty. It's late enough that I almost got up and made my own breakfast. As I was saying, she got a call from Madelaine, you know, the lady who owns the grocery store."

"A gossip."

"And she got a call from Mrs. Thomas."

"That must have made your blood pressure spike."

"Who, as you know, owns the gas station with her husband Fred."

"Oh."

"And she said the most amazing thing. That you and Win were towed back to town this morning in that red car. And you weren't wearing much more than a postage stamp of a dress." Mrs. Kinnear peered at her daughter's noncontroversial linen shirtdress. "And he—Winfield, not Fred—wasn't wearing a shirt. Just a suit jacket. And that isn't even the most shocking part."

"It isn't?"

"No. The most shocking part is that Fred says that when he closed up shop, you two were still at it."

"No, Mom, I think the most shocking part is when I tell you that he asked me to marry him."

"Old news."

"And that he wanted to get married day after tomorrow."

Mrs. Kinnear looked as if she might have scalded her mouth, though she had not taken but a sip of her coffee.

"Did you say yes?"

"Yes, but I need you to say it's okay. Not because I'm a child and need your permission but because I'm a grown woman and I have responsibilities to you and to Teddy."

Mrs. Kinnear wiped her mouth with her linen napkin.

"As it happens, darling, I'm in such a good mood that even the notion of you marrying Win doesn't faze me."

And she held up an envelope. One of the many envelopes that she received during the course of an average week.

"I'm a winner. I'll take Teddy on a cruise."

"Oh, Mother, they always tell you that you're a winner. They're lying."

"Publishers Clearing House never lies."

A wide-bodied yellow school bus came to a halt in the parking lot of Village Hall. Eighteen children of various ages and their uniformly dirty duffels, backpacks, and totes tumbled out of the doors. Mothers—and some fathers who had gotten off work—were waiting with hugs and kisses. Teddy was last to get off. He looked around, waving when he caught Zoe's eye. She had been sitting on a park bench a little apart from the other moms—but she needn't have feared prying questions or nudged elbows, because the return of a kid from camp is such a happy occasion that it trumps even the most delectable gossip.

Teddy hugged her forever and ever when she came up to him.

"You weren't home last night when I called," he complained.

"I'm sorry, honey."

She picked up his backpack. It smelled bad, and she would have told him that he positively couldn't put dirty socks in the pack without waiting for them to dry, but since her experience with Win's car, she was more forgiving.

"Can we go home?" he asked. "I just want to get some sleep. The kids were singing "Ninety-nine Bottles of Beer" all the way."

"Sure," Zoe said. "We're having a welcome-you-home barbecue tonight. You should rest up. I have grocery shopping to do."

"Lemonade," he said when he got into the car. "I mean, love you."

"Love you, too," she said. She turned the ignition.

"Mom, I gotta question for you."

She knew it was coming.

"What is it?"

"Please don't have your feelings hurt when I ask you."

"I won't. Cross my heart."

A heart that was pounding a rapid beat.

"Would you tell me who my dad is?"

She had been anticipating it, but when it came, she wasn't any better prepared than if she had been struck by lightning. Nonetheless, she maneuvered the car out of the village parking lot and got as far as the next intersection without hitting anything.

"I love Paige and Kate," Teddy said. "But give me some credit—they're not my actual, real, biological mom. You can't have three moms."

"They are in a very special . . ."

"I know. In a special way. But not like you. And, Mom, I don't mean to hurt your feelings, but I want to meet my dad."

She parked the car by the curbside. Her hands were shaking. "Teddy, we were very young when we became your mother . . ."

"*You* were very young," Teddy corrected sternly.

"Okay, *I* was very young. I didn't understand how much of a blessing children are. And how they bring people together, not drive them apart. How unexpected gifts can sometimes be the very best kind. I was very scared when I became a mom."

"Because of how people would talk?"

"It was exactly the sort of thing I was most afraid of—people's disapproval. And when Paige and Kate volunteered this idea, I thought it would take the focus off me. And it did. I guess, because I was adopted, I didn't understand how important the biological bond would be."

"Biological bond between me and who?"

"Your father. Teddy, I also needed them because I wasn't sure I would be any good at being a mom."

"But you're the best," Teddy said. "I mean, Paige and Kate are, too. But you're the best."

"But it's easier to be a mom when you have the father's help."

"It's a Skylar brother, isn't it? I hope you won't get mad at me, Mom, but I went to the clerk's office when we toured the courthouse in Vail and, I got some information off my birth certificate."

"I'm not mad. But you didn't need to do that. You could have just asked me."

"Well, I'm asking now. Which brother is it? TJ? Matt? Win?"

"Please. It's a little more complicated than that. We have someone's feelings to protect."

"Whose?"

"Mrs. Skylar's."

"That batty old lady who won't leave her house?"

"Teddy."

"All right, that respected old lady who won't leave her house?"

"Slightly better."

"So, what gives?"

"There were four Skylar brothers. You know Matt and TJ well; they were the youngest."

And so she told him the whole story, as best as he could understand it. Knowing that as he got older, he would understand more. And be told more.

"I admired Jack so much. He was everything a man should be. Strong, brave, hardworking, responsible."

"But did you love him?"

"In a very special way, yes, but maybe not the way a wife loves her husband."

She described in the faintest outlines the accident on the mountain that had shaped their lives. She did not describe how, just weeks after Jack's funeral, she had awakened with morning sickness. How she had gone to Mrs. Skylar, how the grieving mother had accused her of besmirching her eldest son's reputation. How Mrs. Skylar had threatened her with vague harms if her son's name were dragged through the mud. How it had only been in the last several years that she had come to see the widow Skylar as the sad and lonely woman that she was. She downplayed how the accident had affected all of them—TJ, Matt, Kate, Paige, and herself—even these many years later.

And then she thought about how it was Win, always Win, who was on her mind. She pulled the car back out into traffic.

"I only had two wishes. To be a good mother to you. And to be a good daughter to Grandma."

"Aren't you supposed to get three?"

"Life doesn't work out the same way that fairy tales do."

"But you always tell me that I can attain anything I wish for, if I wish hard enough and work hard enough."

"Sometimes people who love each other can work really hard and it still doesn't work out."

"And then what do they do?"

"Spend the rest of their lives regretting."

"Mom, it's a stop sign. And it's your turn."

"Oh, sorry."

"So, why do we have to protect Mrs. Skylar?"

Zoe shook her head, clearing away her thoughts about Win.

"She didn't want to believe that Jack was your father."

"Why?"

"I guess she wanted to believe that Jack was perfect," Zoe said carefully. "Just like I believe you're perfect."

"Mom!"

"Sorry, can't help it. You're so wonderful."

"So, what about Win?"

"That's something important I have to talk to you about."

"That's so weird."

"Marriage? Marriage isn't weird. Marriage is a great bond between a man and woman, and I hope one day you'll find a wonderful woman. I want to marry Win, but I can only do it if you are okay with it. Because as much as I love him, I'm your mom first."

"Do I still get to live with you?"

"Of course, why would you ever think you wouldn't?"

"Well, everything's been changing so fast."

She tousled his hair.

"And one more thing, Mom. I wasn't saying marriage was weird. I was saying that is weird."

He pointed to the Little Lilac window, which was papered over with a single announcement.

"Oh, Lordy."

"Yeah, *oh, Lordy* is right," Teddy said, momentarily forgetting that he was not supposed to take the Lord's name in vain.

On the window of the Little Lilac tearoom was a long, white banner with three words in large, bold-faced print: THANK YOU, WIN.

Zoe stopped the car.

"Mom, what's going on . . . Mom, wait up!"

Zoe ran into the Little Lilac. Mrs. Libby Joyce smiled broadly.

"Hello, Teddy, how was camp? Want a milk shake? Chocolate, right? That's your favorite, isn't it? On the house."

"Yeah," Teddy said, sliding into the first booth. "What's the matter, Mrs. Joyce?"

"What do you mean?"

"You're in such a good mood."

"Teddy," Zoe warned. "Mrs. Joyce, what I think Teddy is getting at is, uh . . ."

"How come she's not in a bad mood?" Teddy supplied.

Zoe sighed.

"And what's with the sign?" Teddy added.

"I'm so sorry, Mrs. Joyce. He needs to remember his manners."

"It's all right," Libby said expansively. "I figured I'd start some talk. But I'm so in love with these new shoes. And it's made all the difference in the world. Funny how pinched toes can put you in a bad mood."

"Did you say *new shoes?*"

"Yes, I did. That Winfield got me some shoes FedExed all the way from Bhutan. They're so comfortable, made out of silk, and I wanted everyone to know that—no matter what you think of Win, even if he's gone to some exotic land—he's all right. You know, he said he'd think of me as his friend from now on."

The screen door opened.

"Lordy, I don't think I ever expected to see you again," Mrs. Joyce said.

Mrs. Skylar entered the tearoom. Her hair was white and piled up beneath a grosgrain-ribboned hat. Her gait was slow, but her posture elegant and stately. She held a pocketbook and a pair of gloves in one hand, and she approached the counter and sat beside Teddy.

"Good afternoon, Libby," she said, as if it had been just a few days, not eleven years, since she had seen the restaurateur. "Mighty hot day, isn't it?"

Libby stared, her mouth opened wide.

"Teddy, this is your . . ." Zoe said.

Mrs. Skylar glanced at Zoe. Her eyes were blue and lined with a turquoise eyeshadow, but the puffy redness of her lids suggested some recent tears.

"Teddy, I am Mrs. Skylar," she said, holding her hand out to the boy. "And I am your grand-mother."

The two shook.

"How 'bout dry toast and tea?" Libby asked. "That always used to be your favorite."

"No, Libby, I'm not in the mood. Young man, what you do suggest?"

"Chocolate milk shake. She's giving them out free."

"My, things really have changed in Sugar Moun-tain," Mrs. Skylar said. "I'll take one, Libby. Make it a large."

Zoe slipped out of the restaurant while the two talked. She found Win standing outside.

"You're not going to believe what—"

He kissed her.

Because he could believe anything now and be-cause he had finally, finally come home to Sugar Mountain, to the woman he had always loved.

Epilogue

"Awfully strange honeymoon," the mayor muttered. He stood at the curb in front of the Kinnear house, leaning against his dark blue Pontiac. The mayor had noticed, in watching television news, that the great urban mayors drove Pontiacs and most had drivers. Sharmaine was driving.

She leaned over the passenger-side seat. She wore her uniform, a navy blue number that nipped and tucked in all the right places. Her hat was white with braiding on its brim. Nice uniform for a chauffeur, in case she gave up the skies.

"I think it's a sweet idea," she said. "If I ever got married . . ."

The revelers began to spill out the front door, a few coming from around back where they had been admiring the Kinnear garden. William Woo offered tiny tulle-and-ribbon bags of birdseed from a basket carried by the lady who ran the bakery—whose name Mayor Stern could never remember though she had been baking éclairs for him for ten years. Sheriff Matt Skylar stepped onto the porch, with

Kate on his arm. He nodded at the mayor. TJ and Paige escorted the Cruikshank sisters to a quiet spot outside the line of traffic. Kurt wore a suit, which surprised the mayor since he had never seen the postman out of uniform.

"I'm holding Win's mail for two weeks," he said to the mayor. "Except if *National Geographic* sends something marked *urgent.*"

The nationally recognized magazine had purchased a collection of Win's photographs of the palace of Thimphu.

"A fancy New York editor wrote him yesterday and said she wants to see his pictures of Kenya," Kurt said. "So, if she sends anything—"

"Don't bother the lovebirds," the mayor warned. "There's been plenty of postal workers who have lost their jobs for snooping."

"Mayor Stern, you wouldn't!"

The mayor's next words were drowned out by the roar of the guests who gathered at the bottom of the front steps. But his meaning was clear—butt out!

Mrs. Kinnear and Mrs. Packer emerged arm-in-arm from the crowd. Mrs. Packer looked better than she had in years, mostly because at the reception she had announced that her son Rory was marrying a girl from Jersey.

"Some kind of contagious disease hitting this country," the mayor said, considering all the weddings he had been invited to over the summer and would be forced to endure through the fall. "Scientists are going to find out this falling in love stuff is caused by viruses."

The two women were dressed in pale blue tea dresses, and they held their pocketbooks over their heads to protect their bouffants from the shower of birdseed. Mrs. Kinnear kissed Kurt on the cheek and told the mayor as he opened the door of the Pontiac that she'd like him to check one more time to make sure that her bags were in the trunk.

"They are," he said. "I promise."

"Check it," she ordered. "I won this Caribbean cruise fair and square and I'm not having lost luggage ruin a good time. You are an elected official and election day is a scant month away."

"I'll get right on that, ma'am."

He opened the trunk, careful not to disturb the ribbons that strung cans and shoes to the fender. All the bags were there. When he slammed the trunk shut, the shouting began again. And from the vantage point of the street, the mayor could see Teddy and his grandmother Skylar emerging from the house. Teddy wore a black suit, and when he waved at the crowd, girls giggled and screamed.

Skylar boy, through and through, the mayor thought. *The whole lot of them are chick magnets.*

Birdseed, raucous cheering, good wishes, and *bon voyage* answered him.

The mayor opened the front passenger-side door and Teddy slid in. Then the mayor helped the elderly Mrs. Skylar into the backseat. He walked around to the driver-side window.

"Take care of them," he told Sharmaine.

"I'll escort them personally to the plane. And I'll make sure the captain knows they're VIP passengers."

"When do you get back?"

"Tuesday," she said, adding, "It's the Denver-Toronto-New York flight."

"Sharmaine, I'm not one for mushy stuff," he said, glancing this way and that to be sure none of his constituents were listening. Wouldn't do for them to know he was a softy. "Could you do me a great honor?"

Sharmaine's eyes widened.

"What would that be?"

"Pick me up a whole case of that champagne. I can't wait any longer. Yeah, I'm serious."

She touched the brim of her cap.

"Will do, Mr. Mayor."

As the Pontiac drove off, Teddy rolled down his window and waved. The crowd cheered, threw rice, waved, and generally agreed amongst themselves that it had been a beautiful wedding at the church and an even finer reception at the Kinnear house.

It was the mayor, and only the mayor, who noticed the front door open just a little. A delicately manicured hand, with a diamond on its ring finger that sparkled just so, curled around the edge of the door and hung a hand-painted sign on the doorknob: JUST MARRIED. DO NOT DISTURB.

"Now that's my kind of honeymoon," Mayor Stern said.

* * *

'Round midnight, the couple got up from the bed in Zoe's room and went downstairs in their pajamas.

"Don't," Win said when Zoe reached to pick up a plate and crumpled napkin that had been left on the living room couch. "We'll do all that tomorrow. Come on. Let's go look at the stars."

He led her out back.

"It's so beautiful," she said, staring up at the heavens.

"Yes, it is," he said. He was looking at her.

"Is he up there somewhere?"

"I think so. He isn't here. Fred explained the stuff about the car—the smell was caused by a break in the manifold intake and the locks were just tight. A little WD-40 and it's good as new."

"And the things we heard and felt?"

"Maybe we drew comfort from believing in them."

"What do you believe in?"

"God. America. Mayor Stern's reelection prospects. And everyone getting three wishes. You only used up two. Maybe Jack couldn't leave until he knew you'd made your last wish."

"I have," she said. "I've got all three wishes."

"Me, too. I just didn't know I was wishing for you." He kissed her. "And you." He kissed her again. "And you." He kissed her again.

"That's not fair! All three of your wishes are the same."

"You have to have known that I, of all people, would be the one to bend the rules."

They kissed, and walked hand in hand back to the house.

Behind them, a single star shot across the black night sky.

BOOK YOUR PLACE ON OUR WEBSITE AND MAKE THE READING CONNECTION!

We've created a customized website just for our very special readers, where you can get the inside scoop on everything that's going on with Zebra, Pinnacle and Kensington books.

When you come online, you'll have the exciting opportunity to:

- View covers of upcoming books
- Read sample chapters
- Learn about our future publishing schedule (listed by publication month *and author*)
- Find out when your favorite authors will be visiting a city near you
- Search for and order backlist books from our online catalog
- Check out author bios and background information
- Send e-mail to your favorite authors
- Meet the Kensington staff online
- Join us in weekly chats with authors, readers and other guests
- Get writing guidelines
- AND MUCH MORE!

Visit our website at
http://www.zebrabooks.com

Put a Little Romance in Your Life With
Fern Michaels

__Dear Emily	0-8217-5676-1	$6.99US/$8.50CAN
__Sara's Song	0-8217-5856-X	$6.99US/$8.50CAN
__Wish List	0-8217-5228-6	$6.99US/$7.99CAN
__Vegas Rich	0-8217-5594-3	$6.99US/$8.50CAN
__Vegas Heat	0-8217-5758-X	$6.99US/$8.50CAN
__Vegas Sunrise	1-55817-5983-3	$6.99US/$8.50CAN
__Whitefire	0-8217-5638-9	$6.99US/$8.50CAN

Put a Little Romance in Your Life With
Janelle Taylor

DO YOU HAVE THE HOHL COLLECTION?